Praise for the
Thomas Martindale Mysteries

Murder at Yaquina Head by Ron Lovell

"Wry, thoughtful, moody, and structured around a secret that reaches back to the era of World War II, Murder at Yaquina Head is a 183 page, gripping mystery which is highly recommended for mystery buffs and would make a welcome and appreciated addition to any community library." *—THE BOOKWATCH*

"...good stuff for a mystery. What really makes it a good read, however, is the self-effacing Martindale, a delightful if sometimes exasperating sleuth who is far too nosy for his own good." *—DENVER POST*

"...Lovell's firsthand knowledge lends an air of credibility to the story and the setting. ...he crafts a convincing story peppered with absorbing details about World War II." *—BOOKLIST*

Dead Whales Tell No Tales by Ron Lovell

"It always seems a little strange to say that a murder mystery is fun. But sometimes they are. Ron Lovell's second venture into the mystery field is a good example. This is a solid mystery with good characters and deft writing." *—STATESMAN JOURNAL*

"Dead Whales is a compelling who-done-it that will keep you guessing until the very last chapter. The characters feel very real—as well-intended and as flawed as the people around us every day. It is a pleasure to read author Ron Lovell's well-crafted prose."
—Clinton McKinzie, author of *Crossing the Line*

"An interesting peek at the politics behind the killing of whales, and a wildly original method of disposing of a murder victim!"
—Carola Dunn, author of the Daisy Dalrymple Mysteries

"Dead Whales Tell No Tales is the second in an enjoyable Oregon-based series starring cranky-but-amiable college journalism professor Thomas Martindale. (Author Ron Lovell knows the turf: He's a professor emeritus of journalism at Oregon State University.)
—SEATTLE TIMES

"An excellent read from an accomplished writer." *—MIDWEST BOOK REVIEW*

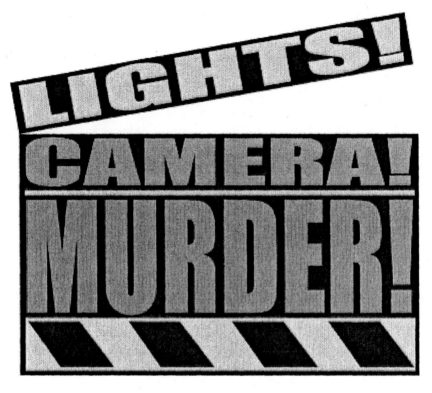

LIGHTS! CAMERA! MURDER!

A Thomas Martindale Mystery

by
Ron Lovell

To Billy Boy and his touchy better half.
I value our friendship.
Love, Ron

SANTA FE

Ron Lovell
7/13/04

*The events, people, and incidents in this story are the
sole product of the author's imagination. The story is fictional
and any resemblance to individuals living or dead is purely coincidental.*

Cover graphic by Liz Kingslien

Sunstone books may be purchased for educational, business, or sales promotional use.
For information please write: Special Markets Department, Sunstone Press,
P.O. Box 2321, Santa Fe, New Mexico 87504-2321.

Library of Congress Cataloging-in-Publication Data:

Lovell, Ronald P.
  Lights, camera— murder : a Thomas Martindale mystery / by Ron Lovell.
    p. cm.
  ISBN 0-86534-425-6 (softcover)
  1. Martindale, Thomas (Fictitious character)—Fiction. 2. Women college
students—Crimes against—Fiction. 3. Television programs—Fiction. 4. Journalism
teachers—Fiction. 5. Oregon—Fiction. I. Title.
PS3612.O84L54 2004
813'.6—dc22
                    2004010061

WWW.SUNSTONEPRESS.COM
SUNSTONE PRESS / POST OFFICE BOX 2321 / SANTA FE, NM 87504-2321 /USA
(505) 988-4418 / *ORDERS ONLY* (800) 243-5644 / FAX (505) 988-1025

To my friends and former students at Oregon State University.
It has been my privilege to know and work with you
during some of the best years of my life.

"There are a thousand hacking at the branches of evil to one who is striking at the root."

— Henry David Thoreau
Walden

1

WEDNESDAY

The door opened and two students entered the classroom ten minutes late. One, a young man wearing a full camouflage outfit and his billed cap on backwards, looked sheepish and virtually flattened himself against the side wall to slink his way to an empty seat halfway back. The other, a young woman wearing a tight-fitting ski jacket, chose to come in by walking directly in front of me, better to be seen by all the class, especially the male members. She selected a seat at the far end of the front row and took off her fur-trimmed parka and unpacked her notebook, pen, and textbook slowly. I resumed my lecture.

"The lead paragraph is the most important thing you will write because it sets the tone for what is to follow. It is the lead that brings readers in and entices them to move on and complete your article. You won't capture the attention of readers if you don't have an interesting and compelling lead."

I stopped because two female students had been talking without hesitancy the whole time I'd been lecturing. As always happens when I pause, everybody looks up to see why. Then they see me glaring at the one or two people making a disturbance and then the class as a whole usually does the same. It works like a charm every time and it worked today.

The two coeds were so engrossed in their whispering, however, that they failed to notice. It wasn't until nearly everyone had turned to face them that they got a clue.

"Are you ladies roommates?"

The bolder of the two spoke first. "Yes . . . we are."

"So you didn't have enough time to say all you had to say to each other before coming to school?"

Both of their faces turned red. "Sorry, professor," said the bolder one.

"We don't assign seats in college—or send errant students to the principal's office. But I have been known to suggest that people go out in the hall to finish their conversations. I won't do that today or suggest that you drop the course."

I smiled as the two sat up straight and looked ready to take notes. Even the guy in the back who had been reading the student newspaper put it away.

"Enough said. Let's get back to the exciting world of lead writing."

I continued to lecture for the next twenty minutes on the different types of leads most people who teach journalism agree need to be taught to the beginner. As I came to each lead, I wrote its name on the blackboard, then read a description. Next, I used an overhead projector to show newspaper stories using the lead in question. Although their textbooks contained the same description and other examples, I've found it best to reinforce this information by repeating it.

"Any questions so far?"

No one moved a muscle. We were halfway through the eighty minute period. It was time to take the class across the hall into the lab room that held thirty personal computers. The students would spend the rest of the class practicing writing the kinds of leads I had talked about this morning.

Everyone gathered up their coats and backpacks and headed over. They sat down and, one by one, started working on the exercise I had placed at each station. The two young women I had criticized sidled up to me in the front of the room before sitting down. They both seemed embarrassed.

"Gol, Mr. Martindale. We didn't mean to make you mad."

"I know, Denise. I just had to make my point. It's a personal hang-up of mine. I get a little angry when I'm trying to explain something up here at the lectern and people in my audience ignore me. How would you feel?"

"Yeah. I guess. We pro'ly shouldn't have done it. We got carried away."

That was Shanda, the other student.

"Boyfriend trouble?"

"How did you know?" said Denise.

They both looked astonished.

"Just a lucky guess."

"That's awesome—I mean that you knew," said Shanda.

I barely managed to stifle a smile.

"I don't hold grudges. I'm glad you see my point. I'm not running a police state. Now, go ahead and take your places. Time's wasting on those exercises. Everybody's got a head start on you."

They seemed relieved and quickly sat down on opposite sides of the room and began to work. After ten minutes or so, I started around to each station to help students write their leads.

"Narrative leads are where you tell a story, like around a campfire."

I leaned down and read what Matt was pecking out on the keyboard.

"Good change."

I moved along to another station.

"Okay. You're doing a delayed lead. You want to entice the reader by the somewhat provocative nature of what you write.

Just then, I heard the trill of a cellular phone. Some student was interrupting my class with news of what—a date, the latest news on who was sleeping with whom? At least, I hadn't been in the middle of a lecture.

The ringing was coming from April Greer's backpack. She was normally a conscientious student. She looked at me like she would rather be anywhere else on the planet than where she was.

"Oh, Mr. Martindale. I'm sooooo sorry."

"Go ahead and answer it!" I said when I reached her desk.

Looking chagrined, she reached into her bag and retrieved the tiny instrument.

"Hello," she whispered.

She listened for a moment, stood up suddenly, then bolted out of her chair as she broke into tears. I moved to comfort her, but her crying turned into a massive wail.

"April. Sit down. Calm down."

I kneeled down to talk to her.

"What is it? Is it . . . your family? Did one of your parents die?"

"Mr. Martindale, they found Emily's body in a dumpster behind her sorority house."

"Emily Morgan. Dead. I can't believe it."

Now I was the one who felt like crying. I had spent the day before with Emily and driven her home last night.

2

PRECEDING DAY

"Quiet on the set. Roll camera and . . . action."

It was interesting to find out that directors really said such things when they were working, not just in movies about making movies. On a drafty sound stage in northeast Portland, a pretty young woman in a cheerleader's sweater stepped forward and began to recite her lines.

"I'm a versatile kind of woman, and I love excitement. Like at Oregon University."

"Cut."

"Professor Martindale. Would people get the wrong idea? I mean the juxtaposition of a cute little cheerleader and the word 'excitement'?"

I didn't answer as quickly as the director thought I should so he pressed the issue. I stepped to the edge of the set and felt every eye in the place on me. Joel Friedkin, wearing ragged jeans and a cutoff University of Oregon sweatshirt, turned to face me.

"What about it, Tom? Is it taboo to use the word 'excitement' in connection with a cute young thing like her?"

Friedkin was leering and I was uncomfortable. The object of our discussion, the young woman, turned red.

"Could we step over there and talk?"

He shrugged his shoulders and we walked off the set, just out of earshot of everyone else.

"Could we ease up a bit on the sexist stuff, Joel? It's making her uncomfortable. And, by the way, she's not a 'thing.'"

"Aren't we being a little uptight today, Tom? You may be her professor, but you aren't her father. I bet she knows more about life than the two of us combined."

"Me anyway," I said, trying to lighten my tone. Even though I was angry, I had to work with this guy for the next month or so. We had to get along. "I'm sure there isn't much you haven't sampled. I know all about you fast movie types."

"Don't I wish all the rumors were true. But you can't be that innocent. Journalists know much more about life than film directors do."

"I left my old dissolute life behind me a long time ago—when I started teaching journalism instead of practicing it."

He leaned in closer, pleased that we had attracted a distant audience for our contrived standoff. He lowered his voice so that the assembled actors and technicians would have to guess what he was about to say.

"Don't tell me you don't wish you could get a little bit of that on the side, Tom."

"We're not here to discuss my fantasy life, Joel. I'd just feel better if you weren't so obvious about her . . . um . . . attributes."

"Whatever."

The director rubbed the stubble on his chin and walked back to the young woman on the set.

"Honey, let's go for another sweater entirely. Patsy," he yelled. "Take her to wardrobe and see what they've got."

A harried looking woman with hair tied back and glasses perched on top of her head came walking in briskly from the other side—his assistant, whom I had met earlier. She smiled at Emily and led her offstage.

"Let's break for lunch," yelled Friedkin.

I looked at my watch. It was almost noon and, by my calculation, we didn't have a usable piece of footage yet and we'd started at ten. I was quickly learning that progress in the film business is even slower than progress in the academic world.

The delay sent everyone to the other end of the sound stage where two women in white aprons were beginning to set up lunch on a long table covered with a glistening white cloth. Even a casual passerby could see that it was a sumptuous feast: roast beef, ham, turkey, various cheeses, five kinds of salads, baked beans, quiche, baskets of bread, and a dessert tray that would make chocolate aficionados weep. No wonder caterers always get printed credit at the end of a film.

Since the university was, presumably, paying for this in its fee to the agency, I plunged in without being invited. After filling my plate with some of almost everything, I walked over to one side of the sound stage and sat down on a wooden footlocker.

"Hey, Professor M. How's it going?"

"Hi, Del. Just barely, I'm afraid."

Delroy Johnson, a black football player from California, laughed as he sat down beside me. He had been in my feature writing course the year before. Even though he isn't a J major, he still dropped by to see me from time to time. He had been asked to appear in this ad series, no doubt to lend his clean-cut persona to the cause of racial diversity.

We both plunged into our meals with the joy that comes from knowing that not only was all of this very good, it was also free.

"So how'd you get into this, Mr. Martindale?"

"The university needs someone to represent its interests here. I'm the liaison to make sure the university's good name is not damaged in any way. I'm supposed to tell the director when things he wants to do are inaccurate or inappropriate. And, I also wrote the script."

"How can you fit this in with all your classes?" he asked.

"I'm teaching one less course this term to give me more time to do this. It's been fun so far, but I hate these delays. I guess we'd all better get used to it. This is just the first day. There could be a lot more like it."

"Hi, professor. Hi, Del. May I join you?"

Emily Morgan, the young woman who earlier had gone to change her sweater, sat down. In contrast to my plate, Emily's contained two slices of turkey and some salad. She noticed me looking at the skimpy fare she had selected.

"I'm trying to lower my intake of fat grams. Lots of things to make you gain in all of that," she said, motioning toward our plates as Del and I laughed at the same time.

"I burn it up in my exercise routine," Del said, running his hand down his perfectly sculpted body.

I didn't follow suit. "I just like to eat, whether I burn it up or not."

We all laughed.

"How's Gabe? Is he staying eligible?" Emily asked Del.

"Just barely I'd guess. Don't see him too much in the off-season."

"I tutored Del's teammate, Gabriel Washington, last season. In writing. I enjoyed it," she said to me.

"He really enjoyed spending that time with you, Emily."

Emily Morgan had been an advisee and student of mine for three years. She was from Medford, a town in southern Oregon. She was a bright, pretty young woman who wanted eventually to work for a TV network news program in New York. I was sure that she had auditioned for this ad assignment to get another work sample for her demo reel.

"Did you mind that hassling from the director?" I dabbed my mouth with a starched linen napkin.

"No, not really. I just let that kind of stuff roll off me. It's something that goes with being a woman . . ."

"An attractive woman," Del interrupted, giving Emily a big smile.

"That may be true, but it was still out of line. Do you want me to say anything more to our friend, Joel? I could do a stronger 'we-don't-do-that-kind-of-thing-on-campus' routine on him."

"No. It didn't bother me, really it didn't at all."

We made small talk until 12:45, when we heard a buzzer and a muffled voice from down at the other end summoned us back to the sound stage.

"Finish up, people. We've got a TV ad to do!" We groaned and returned our real china plates to the beaming caterers still standing by the table.

Emily did fourteen versions of her riff on the university. After seven of them, Joel decided he wanted her to change into an orange and black sweater with a big "O" on the front. While not the precise style worn by cheerleaders, it would at least make the connection better.

Eventually, he was satisfied and sent Emily off to the dressing room to change. She wouldn't be needed again until shooting started on campus next week. As much work as possible was being done here to save money. Filming on location is always more expensive than that done in a studio because of the need to haul people and equipment to the site and keep onlookers out of the way. But some of the shots had to be done on campus to add authenticity to these ads.

Now it was Delroy's turn. Joel snapped his fingers and the hapless Patsy brought the slightly embarrassed young man to a mark on the floor. He was dressed in his football uniform and looked good.

"Let's have a sound check."

A microphone was lowered to a point in front of Johnson's face.

"Not that low, Gordy. Take it up out of camera range!"

The mike all but disappeared as mysteriously as it had appeared.

"Give me your name, please."

"Del Johnson."

"Where you from?"

"Compton, California."

"Tell me a little about yourself, Del."

"I'm a political science major. I hope to go to law school. I like playing football and I have a full-ride scholarship."

"Good, good. That sound okay to you, Gordy? Great. I guess we're ready."

The ever-efficient Patsy held a clapper board in front of the camera. "January 15, 1996. Oregon University recruiting film, take twenty," she said, as she slapped the top into place.

"Let's pull up that accent light, Ralph," said Friedkin. "Now we'll want quiet on the set before we have action."

"I'm a versa-tile kind of guy . . ."

"Cut."

"That's too much stringing out that word. It's pronounced 'versatil'—not 'tile'. Just relax. You're too tight. Take some deep breaths and move your shoulders around."

Del's relaxed demeanor of a half-hour ago was gone, replaced by taut shoulders, clenched hands, and tiny beads of perspiration on his forehead. As he tried to loosen up, a woman with a powder-puff darted onto the set and dabbed at his head and upper lip. He nodded his thanks and relaxed his shoulders.

"Good, good. Okay, Del. We'll have quiet on the set and then action!"

"I'm a versa-til kind of guy and I . . . love . . ."

"Cut. Jesus Christ . . . Leroy . . ."

"Delroy. Del."

"Oh, uh, yeah. Del. You've got to quit screwing up here. This is costing us big bucks."

It seemed strange that Joel had taken Emily through fourteen takes and was now getting angry at Del after only two. What was happening here? Was Joel a racist as well as a male chauvinist?

"Joel. May I have a word with Del?"

It was time for me to do a little "liais-ing."

"Sure, professor. Be my guest. Anything that gets us off this dime. Everybody take ten."

People were mumbling as I walked up to Del and took him by the arm. I steered him to the side where we sat down.

"Del. You've got to calm down. I've seen you get up in front of a room full of people and not be this nervous. What gives?"

"I don't know. Maybe the stakes are higher here. I'm not just representing myself here. I'm representing my . . ." he paused.

"Your race?" I asked gently.

He nodded.

"Maybe that's the problem. Maybe it isn't that earthshaking. These people here aren't judging you on the color of your skin. They want you to do a good job for the sake of the production. They're pulling for you, I know it."

"I . . . guess . . . so. There's something else."

He turned and looked me straight in the eye.

"Seeing Em . . . Emily . . . is hard. Being so close . . . It's hard."

"You could have fooled me. You acted pretty normal."

He turned away and hung his head.

"Yeah. We broke up two months ago."

"I didn't know. So that's making you nervous and causing you to flub your lines?"

"Probably. I thought I was over her but . . ."

"Look, that has to be treated as another issue. We've got to get this shoot over with. I'll take Emily outside with me. That way you won't think about her as much. Then you can say your lines and we can all go home."

"That would help. Thanks, Professor Martindale."

We stood up and walked back onto the set, he straight to his mark, me over to where the director was sitting in a canvas chair, drinking coffee.

"Joel. I think he'll be okay now. Just nerves."

"God, I hope so. I don't want to have to recast him. He's a handsome kid and adds to the diverse look I think we both want for these spots."

He grabbed his megaphone.

"All right, people. Break is over. Let's all move back into position."

Everyone reappeared and a woman darted onto the set to touch up makeup again. Del seemed more relaxed now and was actually smiling.

Emily was watching from atop a large packing crate at the edge of the set.

"That's quite a perch. Can we get some air?"

I helped her down and we walked toward the exit door. We stepped out onto the loading dock, with the traffic on Sandy Boulevard rumbling nearby. Like on most winter days in Oregon, it was raining.

"This going to be too chilly for you, Emily?"

"Nah, Mr. Martindale. I'm tough. Besides, this sweater is wool. I'm comfortable."

"It suddenly got very stuffy in there. I hate the repetition of film work. You can cover up your mistakes by doing them over and over again, but it would be nice to get it right the first time."

"What did you say to calm Del down?"

"I just tried to convince him that the fate of his people wasn't riding on how well he said his lines. I also promised him I'd get you out of his sight."

She looked surprised and hurt.

"He asked you to do that? Does he hate me that much?"

"Hate was not the prevailing emotion here. I think he's still in love with you."

Her face turned red.

"That is nobody's business, certainly not yours. You're a teacher, not a relationship counselor!" she blurted out as she turned and grabbed for the handle on the heavy door behind us. The dampness made the handle slick and it slipped out of her hand, adding to her anger. I quickly stepped over to it, maneuvered the handle, and held the door open for her. She barged through it without looking at me.

As I followed her through the door, I heard Del reciting his lines.

"I'm a versa-til kind of guy and I love adventure. Oregon University. Now there's an adventure."

"Cut and print. Good going, Del. That was the best reading yet. That's it, everybody."

For a change, Joel sounded happy.

In these tough economic times, college recruiting had become intense and competitive—at times, even cutthroat. Private schools especially spent thousands of dollars to entice prospective students. Lavish four-color brochures extolled the virtues of academic programs and the glories of campus life. A few even sent personalized videos to hot prospects at what, for us at public universities, seemed like an outlandish cost.

Until the mid-1980s, the university hadn't had to worry about declining enrollments. The excellence of its programs and the loyalty of alumni brought full enrollment to a campus that was less radical and more traditional than the University of Oregon, its biggest rival, just forty miles up the Willamette River.

So the university sat on its considerable laurels and let the U of O and other colleges in the state out-recruit it. It eschewed clever recruiting materials and flatly refused to run ads on television and radio. Recently, however, enrollment had not met projections and the university had been told to cut millions of dollars from the budget. I only hoped our ad campaign would not be too little, too late.

Joel motioned me over and I sat next to him in an identical canvas chair. We talked as technicians turned off lights and struck the set.

"I'm happy, Tom. Are you happy? I always want to keep a smile on the client's face."

Joel seemed almost jaunty.

"Yeah, I think it's going well. Is the script working out?"

I was trying not to fish for a compliment, but I really wanted to know if what I'd written was practical to film.

"Yes, it is," he answered. "The script isn't bad for one written by a has-been reporter and out-of-touch journalism professor."

He didn't wait for my response to start laughing.

"Has-been reporter and out-of-touch and uptight journalism professor," I replied with a straight face.

"I guess I was being sexist with the girl. She is something to look at though. How do you stand it? I mean being in class with twenty young things that look like her?"

"Well, in the first place, they don't all look like her. More importantly, though, I taught myself a long time ago not to look at my students in that way. If you step over the line it's called moral turpitude. Get charged with that and you're out on your keister."

"Is that like screwing a coed, Tom?"

"You can say that, Joel, yes—but I won't."

We both laughed. If you only knew the truth, I thought.

"Okay, Tom, let's talk about our shooting next week on campus. You know I want general footage of students, teachers, classrooms, and buildings."

"I just need to make some follow-up calls tomorrow to finalize things with the people involved. There shouldn't be any trouble. I don't expect any red tape. The other half of what you want may be a bit harder, but not impossible."

The idea behind the commercials was showing the university as a great adventure—and a diverse one. That meant combining the footage shot here, at different locations, and on campus with archival material. The characters—Del and Emily and others—would react to what was being projected behind them.

"I'd like shark footage . . . having them attack guys in submerged cages and stuff like that."

"We don't do research on sharks."

"Umm. Well . . . jellyfish. They can be colorful."

"Not that either. I can offer you oysters."

"Oysters are boring. Not visual. Besides, they've never been known to attack anyone."

He wasn't smiling.

"Joel, I don't mean to be harsh, but this is not like one of those videos sold on TV of animals killing other animals in savage attacks. This is an ad to get more high school kids to enroll."

"Well, yeah, whatever. . . . What else have you got for me?"

"We do whale research at the Marine Center in Newport. But whales don't attack people."

"Yeah, yeah, I know."

He seemed dejected. Suddenly, his face brightened up.

"What about that guy who was swallowed by a whale a long time ago?"

"Jonah?"

"Yeah, him."

"That wasn't one of our whales. I could get you generic whale footage. I mean of them swimming along and surfacing and blowing water out of blow holes."

"Sounds doable."

"We also do fisheries and wildlife research."

"Grizzly bears. Now they attack people."

"Not our people. Besides, there are no grizzly bears in Oregon. We study smaller kinds. But a mama and her cubs—filmed from a distance—would cause the audience to chuckle."

"Yeah, yeah. Whatever."

It went on this way for some time as I outlined ideas for him. Eventually, we agreed on the whale and bear shots, plus footage of a scientist looking into a microscope (for science), models strutting on a fashion show runway (for apparel design), the trading floor of the New York Stock Exchange (for business), a pharmacist filling a prescription (for pharmacy), artists sketching a nude model (for art), a play in rehearsal (for theater arts), and the orchestra in performance (for music). Even though none of it showed any mayhem, Joel eventually seemed satisfied.

I felt good too because it would show the university's diversity and fit in well with the overall slogan for the ads, "Oregon University: Where Tomorrow's Great Adventure Begins."

We said our good-byes and I gathered up my rain gear and briefcase in preparation to leave. As I walked through the now empty sound stage, I heard loud voices from behind a stack of packing crates.

"You can't do this to me Em! You're making me really mad. I risked a lot to love you. I don't like being called an Oreo! I thought you loved me. Wasn't the sex good enough for you?"

"Sex had nothing to do with it. I don't base my feelings about a relationship on sex. There's more to life than sex. It's just that we don't have enough in common beyond the physical attraction. I've never seen any guy who measures up to you in looks or . . . sex appeal."

"I'm a dumb stud, then. You'd discard me like a used condom."

"Don't be crude, Del. That's beneath you."

"You didn't mind me so much when you were 'beneath' me last year. That was okay then."

"I'm not going to listen to this trash talk. I thought you'd left all that behind in L.A. Don't spoil what we've had by trying to shock me and hurt me with words."

"You walk away from me and I'll hurt you with more than words."

Del grabbed Emily by both shoulders and seemed about to shake her hard. I had planned to tiptoe away unnoticed, but decided I couldn't do that now.

"Is somebody in here? It's time to go home."

When I reached them he had dropped his arms and she was stepping back. Both looked embarrassed.

"Oh, Del and Emily. I thought I heard voices here. Time to get out of here before we get locked in. Anybody need a ride back to Corvallis?"

"Yes . . . I would."

"But Em, I thought you wanted me to take you back." Del didn't look angry anymore.

"It's no trouble. Glad to do it." I was everybody's friend. Mr. Congeniality, just wanting to ignore the tension and get out of here.

"I think I'll go with Professor Martindale, Del."

3

WEDNESDAY

shook my head to clear my thoughts.

As word spread via whisper around the room, many students, both male and female started to cry. Most stood up and crowded around my desk asking questions.

"We've all had a terrible shock here," I said, knowing I had to take charge. "I think it's pointless to continue class today. We'll resume our work next week."

The twenty-one students followed my directions and got to their feet. Spontaneously, we all moved together to form a circle, joined hands, and bowed our heads.

"Thank you all. I encourage you not to keep your grief to yourself. Talk about what has happened. Talk about Emily Morgan. I'll see you next week. Just forget about that homework assignment. We'll pick up the pieces then."

I moved to the door so I could look each student in the eye as he or she walked out. A few of the young men paused to shake my hand. A few young women hugged me.

As the room became quiet, I slowly erased the blackboard and gathered up my lecture notes and books. I walked quickly down the hall which was surprisingly deserted. My office was in the next section of the building through a set of fire doors. I unlocked the door and closed and locked it behind me but did not turn on the lights. I needed to be alone. I sat down at my desk in front of the window to think about what had happened. In a few moments, I looked up a number in the campus directory, then reached for the telephone and dialed.

"Lieutenant Pride, please."

The receptionist at the campus security office connected me to Angela Pride, an Oregon State Police officer who had just taken over command of security on campus, a responsibility the OSP had had for several years. Angela and I were long-standing friends, having first met ten years before in a bizarre situation I had gotten myself into on the Oregon coast. Then, she was Sergeant Pride.

We had dated a few times but our sexual encounters usually ended badly for me. We drifted apart. Hell, I guess we weren't ever really together, except in my mind and—for a brief time—my heart. We had managed to stay friends—at least I hoped so, now that I was calling her out of the blue after such a long time.

"Lieutenant Pride's office."

The secretary sounded briskly efficient.

"This is Professor Martindale in journalism. Is she in?"

"May I ask what this is pertaining to?"

"I need to ask her about the death of one of my stu . . ."

"If you want to report a crime, you must call 9-1-1. This is the director's office."

"I know that, ma'am."

I tried to keep the edge out of my voice by smiling. I was being extra courteous to mask my irritation.

"We're old friends and I need to talk to her. I would appreciate it if you would put my call through."

She put her hand over the mouthpiece and spoke to someone.

". . . says . . . friend . . . Martin something. Sir, your name was . . .?"

"Martindale, Thomas Martindale in journalism."

"Please hold for Director Pride. Thank you for your patience."

Her sudden change in tone probably meant that Angela had walked by.

"Tom. Long time no see. How are you doing?"

"Angela. God, at last! Your secretary is the original gatekeeper."

"Don't be snippy. Bernice was just doing her job. Just a minute while I close my door."

I could hear her chair creak, then footsteps, then a static-filled crackle as she picked up the receiver.

"I know she can be a pain. She thinks she's helping me but she usually just makes me mad. Frankly, I can't wait until she retires at the end of the year. Call my direct line from now on."

She was speaking so low I could barely hear her. I wrote down the number.

"Now, what can I do for you?"

She was speaking normally now.

"I wanted to congratulate you on your promotion and on assuming command of Campus Security. I've been remiss in not calling before this. How long have you been here?"

"Two weeks. I like being around kids and working in such a pretty setting. If I can get all the titles and academic ranks right."

"Yeah, people do get a bit testy about their credentials. Sometime I'll give you a brief lesson, if you want me to."

"I'd appreciate it, Tom. Now, what's really on your mind?"

"I just heard that somebody found the body of one of my students in a dumpster behind a sorority."

"Boy, word travels fast. We've just begun our investigation and haven't released any information. What's your interest, Tom?"

"I've known the student in question for several years. Had her in class, met her family. It's Emily Morgan, right?"

"I'm breaking a rule here, but I'm going to assume I'll be talking to you in the investigation—for background. Let me look at the paperwork here on my desk."

She fumbled with some papers.

"Here it is. Decedent is Emily Jane Morgan, 1325 Borago Drive, Medford, etc., etc. Says here she is a senior, majoring in journalism. Your department, right?"

My eyes filled with tears and my voice cracked when I spoke.

"That's her. I hoped there'd been some mistake."

"How'd you know about this so fast?"

"Her roommate got the news in class last period. It really shook up the kids. How was she killed?"

"A blow to the back of her head."

"Are you handling the investigation?"

"We share jurisdiction with the local police. We'll handle the on-campus stuff; they'll do crime scene and some of the interviews. It's a touchy thing. You know the body was found in an alley behind a sorority house. That's city."

"Yeah, so I heard. Look, Angela, I'd like you to keep me posted on this. I was fond of Emily. In fact, I spent some time with her yesterday."

"*You* spent time with her yesterday?"

4

PRECEDING DAY

"Somehow I didn't ever see you as a sports car kind of guy."

"Yeah, it's a vintage Mustang. I call this my mid-life crisis car."

Emily and I were cruising down the freeway toward Corvallis. She hadn't spoken for the first ten miles or so, just sat and cried quietly. I let her get it out of her system and relax. I found a classical music station on the radio and we just listened.

We were south of the Canby exit before she spoke again.

"I guess you're wondering what that was all about, I mean with Del?"

"Look, Emily, I learned a long time ago when to pry and when to keep quiet. If this was an interview for a story, I'd have started asking questions back on the sound stage."

"I really think . . . I really want to tell you, Mr. Martindale. I need to tell you."

I passed a slow moving truck in the fast lane, then hit the right blinker and eased back in the middle lane, good for cruising along without attracting police attention to a yellow sports car.

"I'm glad to listen. I'll respect your confidence."

She stared out the side window at the occasional lights shimmering from businesses along the side roads. In the fleeting light I could see tears running down her cheeks. We drove along for another few miles in silence.

"We met soon after Del transferred here from a junior college in California. He was recruited by Coach Martino to play football for us."

"Martino. That's a name I've never heard. I guess I only know of the head coach—Brewster, is it?"

"That's right, George Brewster. Ricky Martino is his right-hand man. He's like the first among equals among the assistant coaches. He's in charge of recruiting new players. Some people say he runs the team. I know he spends a lot more time with the players than the head coach does. Everyone assumes he'll move up when Coach Brewster retires.

"Anyway, you were telling me how you met Del."

"We got to know each other when I was working as a tutor for the Step-Up Program."

"That's one university program I don't think I've heard of."

"It's a series of remedial classes to help athletes do better in their courses."

"You mean stay eligible."

"That's not the way coach sees it."

"Well, that doesn't surprise me. I've suspected for a long time that many athletes are recruited by us and other universities just for their abilities on the playing field. The athletic department cares about them only as income producers. Props them up academically so they can play but then drops them when their best days are over. They're treated like raw meat."

I glanced over at her.

"Am I wrong about this? I'm not much of a sports fan but I've kind of kept track of this in the news, because it concerns students."

"No, I guess you're right, at least about some of it, I mean for minority players.

"That's really who I was talking about. I mean they're recruited out of high school and they come up here with the idea of making it big as a way out of poverty, but it seldom happens. And, what's worse, they don't even get a good education. I mean, some of them don't. They're kept eligible by letting them take easy courses."

"Step-Up was designed to help the kids you're talking about. I taught grammar and very simple writing."

"I'm surprised Del was in something like that. He's very articulate. He did well in a feature writing course he took from me."

"He didn't need it, you're right. He came with another player, Gabriel Washington."

"Oh yeah, the guy you and Del mentioned at lunch."

"They've known each other since grade school. Gabe's always looked up to Del. He doesn't do very well in his courses. He's had trouble passing everything since he hit campus. But he's a good lineman so Coach Martino put him in the program to help him do better."

"And Del gave Gabriel moral support."

"He kind of helped me with everyone. Got the guys to quit razzing me in class."

"And you became close because of that?"

"Yeah. He asked me out for coffee, then pizza, then I met him at his apartment and . . ."

"You don't need to fill me in on everything." Emily's candor was making me uncomfortable.

"No, I want to tell you. I've got to tell someone."

"Sorry to interrupt."

"Mr. Martindale, you're a good listener. I'll bet the people you interview really spill their guts."

"Well, I wouldn't go that far," I said, but she was right. All my life, people have confided in me, I guess because I don't come across as very threatening. This had been a godsend to my reporting career.

"Whatever. So we began seeing one another pretty steadily. I live in a sorority so we had to meet at Del's house. I'd go there in the afternoon and fix dinner and we'd study together and . . . you know."

"I don't want this to sound insensitive but how did other people react? I mean people can be pretty narrow-minded.

"My family freaked-out, absolutely. My dad thinks he's a liberal but when it came to his only daughter dating a black man, he forgot all of his old beliefs. We had a huge fight last Christmas when I wanted to bring Del home. My dad even resigned from the Medford Human Rights Council when I called him a hypocrite."

"And your mom?"

"She died last year of breast cancer."

"I'm sorry. It's really hard to lose a parent."

We drove in silence for another mile or so.

"Do you have brothers and sisters?"

"One younger brother, Billy. He's in high school. He likes football so much that the thought of having a player of any race in the family is cool with him."

"How about your friends?"

"The close ones understand, and the others—I don't care about them. I'm thinking about moving out of the sorority anyway. Because I broke up with Del, my dad has said he'll pay for an apartment."

"Did you break up to cool things off at home?"

"Never. I wouldn't give in to a bribe. My dad knows that. No, it was just that I decided Del and I didn't have enough in common to have a permanent relationship. I guess you heard us arguing?"

"Yeah. I'm afraid so. It was hard not to."

"He said I dated him for sex. That really hurt me. I thought we were together because we loved each other."

"What about Del? What was he going through?"

"The same kind of stuff—from other sources. For one thing, the coach freaked out like my dad. Yelled and screamed at Del, threatened to throw him off the team if he didn't break up with me."

"Why such a violent reaction?"

"He's always worried about the image of the team, so I guess it was partly a PR thing. And Coach Martino knows my dad. I used to baby-sit his kids my freshman year. I think he was trying to protect me. He even sent his wife to talk to me."

"His wife? Coach Martino involved his wife in this?"

"Yes. She's very involved with the team. Travels with them, has them over to dinner, that kind of thing. She has always taken a particular interest in minority players. She cares about them a lot."

I put on the right blinker as I spotted the exit sign for Albany, the mill town ten miles northeast of Corvallis. I downshifted as we sped off the freeway onto Highway 99E. We were twenty minutes from the Corvallis city limits.

"You want to stop for some coffee?"

"That would be nice."

I pulled into a McDonald's, placed our order, then drove around to pick it up and pay. Then, I parked in the main lot. No need to get third degree burns on my legs from spilled coffee.

"I wanted to ask you a few more things before we drop the subject. What about the reaction of Del's friends and family? I mean to the two of you getting involved?" I asked, taking a sip of coffee.

"His parents are dead. He was raised by his grandmother and I think she died recently, too. So I guess there wasn't any reaction from whatever family is left. He never talked about it. Up here, he said some of the white players didn't think he should see me. I guess Gabriel got mad at him too."

"Your tutorial student?"

"Yeah, his old friend."

"What happened?"

"He went completely ballistic one night after practice and yelled and screamed at Del for getting involved with me."

"How did all of this affect your class?"

"I decided to quit teaching in the Step-Up program. Too many people were having a problem with me. I guess I asked too many questions about cheating I'd heard about. I just didn't need the grief. I've been concentrating on . . ."

"Cheating? What kind of cheating? If that happens the whole team will be ineligible to play–am I right?"

"I don't know much . . . I've probably said too much already." She looked frightened and quit talking. I dropped the subject.

We finished our coffee and drove most of the rest of the way to Corvallis absorbed in our own thoughts. I pulled up in front of her sorority at about eight p.m. She got out, slung her bag over her shoulder, and leaned down, her head protruding slightly through the open window.

"I want to thank you for listening. I didn't mean to bore you."

"I was glad to listen. Anytime. I'll see you for the shooting next week on campus.

She smiled slightly and walked up the brick path to the columned facade of the sorority house. I waited until she was safely at the door. As she entered, she turned around and waved.

5

WEDNESDAY

"You drove her home yesterday? We need to talk in person right now. Where is your office? I'll be right over."

"I'm in Ag Hall two twenty-four."

"Where is Ag Hall? I haven't sorted out the geography of this place yet."

"East of the Student Union, next to the bookstore parking lot."

"I'll find it. Wait for me, Tom. Don't talk to another soul."

"Okay, Angela. I'll be here."

As I sat in the semi-darkness of my office, it suddenly dawned on me that I might be considered a suspect. The fact that I had been with Emily Morgan so much of yesterday would make me someone to question. But any connection between me and this murder was ridiculous and I'd be able to make Angela see that. No need to panic. Best to just sit and wait calmly.

I picked up the graded assignments I had forgotten to hand back to the class and straightened them into a neat pile. I then got up and put today's lecture notes into a file folder. I was still mechanically tidying up when I heard an authoritative knock on my outer door. I walked through the small conference room and stopped to listen.

"Who is it?"

"Open the door."

Angela, looked crisp in her neatly pressed blue-gray uniform. I could always count on her to be extremely neat. As a matter of fact, that was one of the things that had come between us. I'm no slob, but I could never get used to her habit of smoothing the rug after I walked on it or doing the dishes right after we finished eating. In time, it became laughable—to me, but never to her. She reminded me of what another friend once said about his wife: she was so neat that when he got up in the middle of the night to go to the bathroom, she made the bed. I never told Angela that old saw, however.

Her leather belt and holster squeaked as she came in. She was taller than I remembered, even when she took off her hat. I glanced up and down the hall before I closed the door. Luckily, no one was around. The last class change had taken place fifteen minutes before. I re-locked the door. We didn't need any interruptions.

"Sit down, please. You look great."

We shook hands. This didn't seem the right time to kiss her, even platonically.

"Nice place. Very cozy. This furniture looks vintage."

"Yeah. Real oak. I've tried to round up some old pieces to fit the building. It was built in 1909. Better than gray metal, don't you think?"

"Definitely."

"It's good to see you again, Angela, even in these terrible circumstances. I wasn't sure we'd ever see one another again after the way we broke up. When I think back, I don't know whether to laugh or cry. It was really embarrassing and I . . ."

"Let's not dredge all of that up now, Tom. Let's cut to the chase. You kind of caught me off guard when you called. I was surprised to hear your voice after all this time. It's best if we stick to business. Tell me what you know about Emily Morgan."

"She's been a student in this department since her freshman year," I replied with a sigh. "She was also my advisee. I'm coordinating an advertising campaign that the university is preparing to attract new students."

"Coordinating?"

"A Portland production company is actually shooting the footage."

"So how does—did—Emily figure into this?"

"I picked her as the female lead, you might say. She and a male student recited dialogue about their experiences as students here. That will be combined with narration and film footage about our programs."

"So you talked to her there on the sound stage?"

I nodded, beginning to wonder how I would deal with the issue of Delroy Johnson, if, or when, it came up.

"Any other students involved in this project?"

"On campus next week the camera crew will be filming in classrooms. Several kids will have speaking parts. Or that was the plan before this happened."

"No, I mean up in Portland. Any other students up there?"

I hesitated and Angela picked right up on my hesitation.

"Are you protecting someone here, Tom?"

"Del Johnson. Delroy Johnson is also appearing in the ads."

"The football player?"

I nodded.

"What's he got to do with this?"

"Nothing that I know of. He was just there. You asked me who else was there from here."

"Did they know one another—he and Emily?"

"I gather they used to be lovers."

"Why did she tell you that? I mean you just don't start chitchatting about a thing like that all of a sudden."

I didn't want to say what I knew I had to say.

"I overheard the two of them arguing at the end of the day."

I didn't want to say more.

"Did he threaten her?"

"Not really. He . . ."

Angela stood up and picked up the telephone.

"Pat? Angela Pride here. I want you to look up the address of a person of interest in this Morgan case. Delroy Johnson. Let's pick him up. We might need backup. He's a black kid. Football player. Okay. See ya soon."

She smiled as she put on her hat.

"Angela. Let me explain what happened," I said urgently.

"That's all I need now. Come in tomorrow and we'll take your statement."

6

Quiet settled around me the moment Angela walked out the door. I had managed to implicate Del Johnson in something he may not have had anything to do with. I had probably cast suspicion on the wrong person. Even though I had heard his argument with Emily, I knew Del well enough to be certain that he couldn't have killed her. But a little voice in my head whispered "Are you really sure?"

I shook off my doubts and looked up his phone number in the student directory. My heart pounded as I waited for him to answer and weighed once more the implications of what I was about to do.

"Yeah."

Johnson sounded sleepy.

"Del. It's Tom Martindale. Just listen carefully to what I'm going to say. The police are on their way to arrest you on suspicion of Emily's murder."

"What the fuck? Emily? Murdered?"

"Just get out of there."

| | |

Del Johnson lived on B Avenue, an area of older homes south of campus that had been turned into rooming houses and apartments. As I turned off of Western Avenue, I ran into a police barricade.

"You'll have to turn around, sir. Police emergency."

A young Corvallis policeman wearing a helmet and a flak jacket over his regular uniform leaned into my open car window.

"I am trying to locate Lieutenant Pride of the state police. I'm a witness in a case she's investigating. She may want to see me."

"Pull over there and wait. I'll call it in and see what she says. Your name, please."

"Tom Martindale."

He nodded and walked toward his car a few feet away. He sat down behind the wheel. I couldn't hear what he said, but soon various staccato bursts were coming from his radio. After several minutes, he walked back to my car smiling.

"She says you're a damn idiot to be down here but to let you through. Pull over there in that vacant lot and then walk to the command post just around the corner over there. She's set up in the side yard of that green house."

"Thanks, officer. I appreciate your help."

I pulled into a weed-covered lot that was also plagued by deep ruts and a lot of mud. Following the officer's directions, I turned the corner and headed for the green house. It had a fenced yard on one side. Angela was standing in the open gate, motioning for me to come toward her.

"What you're doing here, Tom? This is police business and has nothing to do with you."

"I thought it might ease the tension if Del Johnson saw a friendly face."

"Jesus Christ, Tom. This man may be a murderer. The last thing I care about is to ease his tension and let him see a 'friendly face.' You're not on one of your amateur detective kicks again, are you? That's the last thing I need to deal with right now."

"I know him. He's a student. I'm concerned about him. I also feel a bit guilty."

"Guilty! You gave me important information. If you hadn't, I'd be after you for withholding material information somewhere down the line."

How about aiding and abetting? I thought to myself.

"Look, Angela. I'm here. Just let me stay and watch. I promise to be quiet and stay out of the way."

"Okay. Put on this flak vest and helmet."

"This is a college kid, Angela. Not Charles Manson."

"Tom." Pride held up one hand." Don't start! What did I just say? And what did you just agree to do?"

I nodded and made a zip-like motion with two fingers.

I had only seen police tactical operations in the movies. But the real thing was not all that different. The *ad hoc* force seemed to be made up of both Corvallis police and state troopers from the detachment assigned to campus. Angela was clearly in charge of the twenty or so men milling around the yard. The house next to it appeared to be empty, as did all the other buildings. Somehow, in the short time since Angela had decided to arrest Johnson, these men had apparently evacuated the entire neighborhood.

Angela was conferring with the men in hushed tones and talking into a radio. After several minutes, the men moved out of the yard in two lines, one going in one direction, the other in the opposite way.

When they had left the yard, Angela motioned me over to a section of fence that had been removed. From there, you could get a clear view down the street.

She put her fingers to her lips as I joined her at the fence. I nodded and looked through the opening. The house where Del Johnson was living was in the middle of the block, set back from the street and smaller than the buildings around it. As with most places students chose to live, it was rundown and needed a paint job. Like in many college towns, some landlords in Corvallis love to collect big rents from their student tenants, but are seldom willing to do much else.

The force advanced so stealthily down the street that I could barely see them. Del Johnson wouldn't have a clue if he hadn't gotten out. Poor kid.

"Ready on right."

A staccato burst broke the silence.

"Ready on left."

Then another.

The men were in place.

Angela motioned to me.

"Stay put."

I nodded and moved back to the opening as she walked out the gate, followed by two troopers holding black shields.

This was getting way out of hand and there wasn't anything I could do about it. I had caused all of this but I was now powerless to do anything to stop it.

Angela walked purposefully down the middle of B Avenue, a bullhorn in hand. She was being protected by the shield-carrying officers walking on either side of her. She stopped behind a large oak tree in the front yard of the house next to the target house and put the bullhorn to her lips. She shouted something, but no sound came out, only a loud electronic screech.

Angela looked disgustedly at the horn, then appeared to shake it and flick a switch on the side several times. This time, it worked.

"Delroy Johnson! This is the Oregon State Police! We have your house surrounded! Take off your shirt and shoes, and come out with your hands on your head!"

From high overhead, I thought I heard a crow cawing. The rumble of the traffic from Highway 20 was audible in the distance.

Angela repeated her command several more times, but each declaration was met by silence. She waited for several more minutes before speaking into her radio. It sounded like she said "now".

The troops instantly advanced on the small house from all directions, quickly forming a perimeter. They were all carrying shields for protection. A cop at a window on the side suddenly broke the glass with his rifle and threw a tear gas canister inside.

Two cops on the sides now advanced on the door, both wearing gas masks. Two others joined them, holding a battering ram. It took only two blows for the ancient wooden door to give way. The four cops at the door and several others from the yard sprinted toward the house, quickly donning gas masks.

The whiff of gas reminded me of an anti-war demonstration I had covered in the past.

I could hear various things being smashed inside over the next few minutes. We all waited for another moment or two. I held my breath, hoping Del hadn't been badly hurt.

One of the men then appeared in the doorway, shaking his head.

Del Johnson had escaped.

7

When it seemed safe to do so, I walked out from behind the fence and started down the street towards Angela Pride and the rest of the officers. I felt a combination of anger and relief. I was glad Del Johnson had gotten away. But I was angry that it had come to this kind of confrontation. Angela Pride was a fair person, but she had certainly overreacted in this instance. I was also very angry at myself for causing all this in the first place. I should have kept quiet. But this second guessing didn't do Del Johnson much good now.

"He got away?" I shouted.

Pride nodded and said something in her radio that sounded like, "All units stand down." She motioned for the policemen to let me through the perimeter. The house was a mess, many of its windows broken and the front door hanging from one hinge. I'm sure it would also be uninhabitable for a while because of the tear gas.

"Someone tipped him off. I'm putting an APB out on him."

"Isn't he only a suspect?"

"Yeah. They were lovers. They broke up. They were arguing. That makes him a guy I want to question. We call someone in that position a person of interest."

I looked at the large number of troops packing up their gear and Del's sad and partially ruined little house, then at Pride.

"I know what you're thinking, Tom. You think I overreacted. It's standard procedure to exercise extreme caution when dealing with a suspect in a murder investigation."

"Forgive me for saying this, Angela, but would you have been as zealous if the student had been white?"

The moment I spoke, I regretted what I had said. A look of fury darkened her face, but she composed herself before replying.

"I'm going to forget you said that, Tom," she said coldly. "I know you are upset over the death of your student. Why don't you go back to your office and calm down?"

I felt immediately contrite. I knew Angela Pride to be a good person and I had been wrong to imply that she had been prejudiced in her reactions.

"I'm sorry, Angela. This is police business and I'll leave it up to you. But I repeat what I said before, Del's a good kid."

"A kid who ran away."

"With all due respect, Angela, maybe he's in class on campus or at the library or the athletic department."

"We checked his schedule before we came over here. He doesn't have any classes today. We'll send a plainclothes detective around to check out the other places."

"Can I ask you a question about your investigation?"

"You can ask."

"Do you have any leads at all in Emily's murder?"

"What you told me about her failed relationship with Johnson is all we've got. I'll know more tomorrow after I get the autopsy results."

"I wish you luck. She was a great person and didn't deserve to have her life end this way—or this soon. I'd better be going. One last question: am I any kind of suspect—or person of interest as you put it?"

"I was just interested that you'd been one of the last people to see her alive. We talked to several of her sorority sisters who saw her come back to the house and a car matching a description of yours drive away. You have a Mustang. Right?"

"Yes I do, Lieutenant. It's parked just outside your perimeter here."

"Kind of racy for a middle-aged guy like you, isn't it Tom?"

Pride was chuckling as she talked.

"Yeah, I tell people it's my mid-life crisis car."

Just then, another state police officer walked over and whispered something in her ear. She turned to me.

"Something's come up. Johnson may have to answer to other charges besides murder."

"What do you mean? What else?"

Angela put up her hand to stop my questions.

"I can't say any more, Tom."

"Still friends, Angela? In spite of what I said?"

She shook my hand and smiled.

III

As I entered my office twenty minutes later, the phone was ringing.

"Is this Tom?"

"Yes."

"Hi. It's Joel Friedkin."

"Yeah, Joel. Hi. I've got some bad news."

"I heard about it on the radio. Too bad. Poor kid. Quite a looker too. Very sexy."

"God, Joel."

"I guess . . . I just say what I think too often."

"I guess so."

"We need to figure out what we're going to do here. We'll need to re-shoot her scenes fast. I'm trying to keep your limited budget in mind. We can get an actress who looks like a coed. In fact, my girlfriend . . ."

"No, Joel. No girlfriends or actresses. This has got to be authentic all the way. When do you want to do the re-shoot?"

"I'd love to do it next week when I'm on campus for that exterior stuff. We can do it there if you can get me into a studio with a seamless backdrop. I can use a hand-held camera and fewer technicians. It'll work, I think. If not, we can do it up here in Portland later. That sound good to you, Tom?"

I couldn't believe that this sometimes difficult man was being so obliging.

"Great. I can arrange for you to use the portrait studio here in the journalism department. We use it for our photography program. It's got a seamless background too. I'll get you a new model."

"What about the black kid?"

"Let's keep everything else the same—for now."

I had already done enough to Del Johnson's reputation without defaming him still more. Others would be doing that soon enough. If we had to, we could deal with the issue of replacing him later.

"Tom, there's one other thing I wanted to mention. Do you know a Charles Gates?"

"He's assistant to the director of public affairs at the University of Oregon. Why do you ask?"

"Well he's been nosing around up here. Asking questions of the crew. They didn't tell him anything."

"What kind of questions?"

"About the ad campaign—what it's about, the theme. That kind of thing. He was even talking to that girl who got killed."

"Gates talked to Emily?"

"One of my guys said he saw it."

"Hmm. Very strange and interesting. Maybe I'd better tell the police. I don't understand all his sneaking around. The U of O has had a good ad campaign for years—better than anything we've done. I'm surprised if they're worried. It astounds me that he'd be so open about it. I'll look into it. Thanks for telling me. I mean you even forgot your old school loyalty and all that."

"What do you mean?"

"The U of O sweatshirt you wore the other day."

"That didn't mean anything. I just like sweatshirts from different colleges. I've got one from Tulane on today. I didn't go there either. My loyalty is to my clients."

"Sorry. I didn't mean to doubt you."

"That's okay, Tom. Well, I've gotta run. I'll be there by nine next Monday morning. If you run into problems arranging things, call me. Otherwise, I'll see you then. Oh, by the way, where's your office?"

"On the second floor of the Ag building, room two twenty-four. Just come to the main gate. I'll arrange parking for you. How many vehicles?"

"A large motor home and a van. See you then."

I hung up and sat staring out the window at the library across the street. Maybe Joel would turn out to be a good guy after all. It was a real surprise to discover that U of O would deign to care about our ad campaign. I opened the drawer in my desk and took out a file marked University Advertising Campaign. It held one of the few copies of the script. I put it in my briefcase for safekeeping at home. I'd be damned if somebody from the PR department of our biggest rival was going to get a preview of what we were planning to do. They'd have to see it along with the rest of the world.

I spent the rest of the afternoon making arrangements for next week's filming. I arranged with the drama teacher who directs most of the university productions to interview three replacements for Emily tomorrow. With our tight timetable to get the ads on the air, we couldn't waste any time.

I also ran all this by Hadley Collins, the vice-president for public affairs and my boss on this project. She readily agreed with what I proposed.

I left her office about six and drove home. It had been an exhausting day and I was beat. I needed a hot shower, a glass of wine, and the piece of the lasagna I had in the refrigerator. I soon pulled into the carport behind my condominium in the Timber Hill section of town.

As I approached the back door, I noticed a piece of paper sticking under it. So much for the tightness of my weather-stripping. I bent down, picked it up, opened the door, and turned on the light.

I put my briefcase on the table and unfolded the note.

If you want to halp Del Johnson, folo me now.

It was signed Gabriel Washington. Del's friend, the kid Emily had been tutoring.

I looked around as the driver of a Ford pickup flashed its lights from the adjacent parking area. As nonchalantly as I could, I picked up my briefcase, turned off the lights, locked the door, and got back in my car.

8

followed Gabriel Washington out of my condominium complex, then turned left on Walnut Boulevard. I reassured myself that this might be impetuous, but not really all that rash. In the first place, I knew Del and didn't think I was in any danger, no matter how desperate he and his friends might be feeling. Also, I wanted to believe in Del's innocence and needed more information to help prove it.

At the first signal, Gabriel pulled into the right lane and slowed his truck down. I pulled alongside and glanced over at him to see him looking back at me.

When I had a clear view of him in the flickering lights from stores in the shopping center we were passing, I nodded once. He acknowledged my sign and sped away, once again getting in front of me.

After taking several zigzag maneuvers through residential streets, we reached Highway 20. When we turned left, I decided we were headed to Portland via Albany. We drove through town, then got onto Interstate 5 heading north. We stayed on the freeway for the next thirty minutes, then exited on Commercial. Soon, we were driving toward downtown Salem.

Gabe slowed his truck and turned on his right blinker. We were now on a narrow street in an older residential area of rundown houses. After two blocks, Gabe pulled up in front of a small house set back from the street on a weed-covered lot. As we got out of our cars, the door opened a crack and someone peeked out.

"Thank you for coming, Mr. Martindale," Del Johnson said. "I really need a friend right now."

He looked quickly at the hulking Gabe standing nearby, and added, " . . . another friend."

Del looked terrible: puffy, red eyes and in need of a shave. His arm trembled slightly as we shook hands. He seemed very distraught

"You're shaking, Del. It's freezing out here. Can we go inside?"

He folded his arms across his chest and hunched his shoulders.

"I can't seem to get warm since I heard about Em."

He stepped aside and we walked into the house.

"Whose place is this?" I asked.

"Gabe's sister, Shawntalla. She usually lives here with her kids, but they're all in California for a while.

"You think you're safe here?"

Del nodded. "For a few days maybe. I'm keeping a low profile and Gabe's bringing me food. There are other black folks living around here, so I don't stand out like I would in a lot of towns in Oregon."

Gabriel Washington uttered a sound for the first time.

"Want a soft drink?"

"That would taste good."

Del slumped in his seat next to me and crossed his legs, the lace from one of his expensive sneakers dangling loose.

"So what happened, Del? How'd you get away from your house so fast?"

His face broke into a big smile, the first time I had seen him at ease all evening.

"I took the secret tunnel."

"Secret tunnel? You're kidding."

"Not at all. The owner of the house is a real nice science professor who supports athletics and tries to help black athletes especially, because he thinks we have a hard time finding a decent place to live in Corvallis."

"Yeah, you got that right!" Gabe grumbled between gulps of his Pepsi and mouthfuls of potato chips.

"So what's he got to do with a secret tunnel?"

"When he showed me around the day I moved in, he mentioned that the previous owner was a graduate student in physics who paid his way through school by raising and selling marijuana right in that house."

"That's what the police must have found."

"What do you mean?"

"When I was talking to a lady cop I know after they raided your house, she seemed . . ."

"You were there?"

"Yeah. After I called you, I couldn't stay away. I drove over to see if I could help you somehow."

"I appreciate it."

"Anyway, the police seemed to find something when they searched the house, but they wouldn't tell me what. Were there signs of pot growing down there?"

"No, the guy took his plants with him when he graduated and moved away. There were still some old fluorescent lights and long wooden tables. I never went down there much."

"What about the tunnel, Del?"

"The place has a small door behind some shelves at the end that leads to a tunnel which connects to an abandoned part of the old Corvallis sewer system. You squeeze through the tunnel and pretty soon you're able to stand up and walk a half mile or so to another opening near the train yard. I was out of my house and in that yard in less than fifteen minutes. Gabe was there with his truck and we were on our way fast."

"You really have the police guessing. They can't figure out how you got away."

He smiled again as he recalled his ingenious escape.

"Before you put your arm out of joint in patting yourself on the back, Del, you need to face some reality here and think about turning yourself in to the police. Not only do they suspect you of murder, but now they may think you're a marijuana grower."

Gabriel Washington jumped to his feet and came stomping over to me, all six foot six inches, three hundred pounds of him. He stood over me for a minute or so, glowering down.

"Let's get one thing straight, man. Del ain't turning himself in."

He turned to Del.

"I told you he was like all the others. He don't care about you, man. He don't care at all."

I cleared my throat. "I do care, Del. I think you know that or you wouldn't have wanted me here. I want to hear what you have to say. It would be much easier—" I looked at Washington with my most withering glance "—if your friend here would go back to his Pepsi and chips."

Del took Washington by the shoulders and gently inched him back away from me.

"Chill out, bro. Go get some more food. There's lots to eat."

The hulking young man relaxed a bit and started out of the room.

"Sorry, man. You too, professor. I get carried away sometimes."

"It's okay, Gabe. I'll be all right."

Del resumed his seat beside me and we continued to talk, this time in more hushed tones than before.

"Gabe's been my friend since grade school in California. He's always been bigger and taller and stronger so he thinks he has to protect me. He takes it too far sometimes, like he said."

"I understand. But his outburst aside, that doesn't change the truth of what I said. If you keep running, things will only get worse for you."

"But I didn't kill Emily, Mr. Martindale. I loved her."

His eyes filled with tears.

"Maybe you loved her in the past. What I saw up in Portland on that sound stage didn't look like a pleasant conversation between two people in love. You were mad."

His face became flushed and he hung his head, sighing before he answered.

"I know how that looked to you. Bad. But it wasn't that way between us. We still cared a lot for each other. I just kind of blew up that she was acting so cold to me. Like strangers. It was a cheap shot for me to say that racial stuff. She hadn't ever let that affect our relationship before. She even stood up to her dad."

"She told me."

"She told you that we were . . . together. I mean . . . as a couple?"

"And how her family objected and she broke it off because of the pressure."

"We split up, but I never got over loving her."

His eyes filled with tears and he turned his head to the side in a vain attempt to hide his grief.

"I believe you, Del."

And I thought I really did. This did not look like an act—and I'd seen some good ones in my journalistic heyday.

"Please help me, Mr. Martindale. I really need you. I just don't know where else to turn."

"You need to go to the police and lay out the whole story. I'll go with you."

"I can't do that. I've seen what happens to black men who go to the police."

"This isn't L.A. or Compton, Del. It's Corvallis, Oregon, for God's sake!"

He didn't answer but I could tell by his silence that he probably didn't believe me.

"Okay, I'll try to help you, but you've got to tell me everything. Maybe we can figure out what to do after that."

Looking relieved, he wiped his eyes with a handkerchief and sat back, ready to talk.

"I was real pissed that she wouldn't ride back from Portland with me—that she preferred your company. But at least it wasn't with a guy her own age, I mean that she might date or something."

He looked sheepish and glanced nervously at me. I know I seemed ancient to my students. I waved away his concerns.

"So I drove straight home and was looking over my notes to get ready for a lit test, when Emily called. She apologized and I apologized and we both decided we needed to see each other right then."

"What time was this, approximately?"

"I'd say eleven or eleven fifteen. The news was on TV. I remember that. So I told her I'd pick her up, but she suggested we meet for coffee at that all-night place on Ninth?"

"Lots of kids go there to hang out and study. The manager is cool. He doesn't get all bent out of shape when more than two black men come into his place and maybe get to jive'n a little too much, or talking a little too loud."

"So you met and talked. A lot of people saw you in there?"

"Yeah. Some we knew, some we didn't. But they'd remember us too, because some of them looked horrified because a black man and a white woman would even be talking together. You know that type."

"Yeah, I suppose I do. Corvallis isn't really a racist town."

"Anyway, we met . . ."

"How did she get over there?"

"One of her friends from the sorority, I guess. Emily didn't have her own car."

"So someone else knew the two of you were meeting?"

"You mean, like a witness?"

"Yeah, but not in a way that would do you any good. That girl, whoever she is, is one more person to tell the police the two of you were together the night Emily was murdered."

He looked defeated.

"I didn't think of it that way."

"Well, you'd better get yourself into a more defensive frame of mind, Del. People are out to hang this on you; you can count on that. Anyway, go on."

"We decided our breakup had been caused by other people reacting to us as an interracial couple—her father, some of my teammates. We both said that was their problem, not ours. We were going to go kind of slow at first—a movie, dinner. You know, nothing heavy, like . . ."

"Sex?"

"Yeah. Maybe a kiss goodnight. We both decided we wanted it that way. We both agreed we'd rushed into things too fast before. We were going to take it slow this time and maybe things would work out better."

"So how long were you there?"

"'Til about twelve thirty. We both had classes today so we needed to get some sleep. I paid the tab and we left."

"Did a lot of people see you leave? I mean would anyone there have a fix on the time?"

"You mean as a sort of alibi for me?"

"Or a witness for the police."

"Some black guys on the team, Bobby Hardy, a white player, and I guess Mrs. M."

"Mrs. Martino?"

"Yeah, she often comes in to have coffee with the guys and help them with their homework, stuff like that."

"You're telling me that Coach Martino's wife spends time in a public place at night with a bunch of football players? Where's her husband while all of this is going on?"

"Oh, maybe out of town recruiting or home working on the play book or something."

"Let me stop you for a minute. You keep mentioning Martino, but what about the head coach . . . a . . . what's his name, Brewster?"

Del nodded.

"You see, Coach Brewster really lets Martino run the team. Nobody says it out loud, but Brewster is really a figurehead, kept in his job by a couple of powerful alums who give so much money to athletics that they can get whatever they want."

"But what's in it for Martino? Couldn't he get a head coach's job—and pay—someplace else?"

"I'm not really sure why he stays. I guess it's pretty certain he'll get the top job in a few years when Coach Brewster retires. And he and Mrs. M really like Oregon."

"That all makes sense. Sorry for the interruption. You were talking about Mrs. Martino. Boy, I'll bet she's a hot topic of conversation when faculty wives meet!"

"You mean because she tries to help black students who have a tough time in school?"

"Look, Del. It may look harmless to you and it may very well be harmless—an act of mercy and kindness for all I know. I'm just saying that it looks strange, especially to a bunch of women who would love to gossip about one of their fellow wives during a game of bridge. It gets pretty savage at times."

"Yeah, I guess."

"Let me ask you something else about Mrs. Martino. Did she talk to you both?"

"You mean that night?"

I nodded.

"I went over to the table where she was sitting with Bobby and Kurt . . . Kurt Blake is her nephew. He's with her a lot. We all said hello."

"Did Emily go over to the table too?"

"She hung back over by the cash register."

"Did Mrs. Martino seem agitated about seeing you two together?"

"No, I don't think so. She said something about being surprised to see us back together."

"Let me ask you something else, Del. How can I say this so you don't get angry? Did Mrs. Martino ever . . ."

". . . try to have sex with me?"

I nodded.

"She kind of hinted soon after we met that she and her husband had an understanding and that it was okay to sleep with other people. She hinted and I played dumb. I knew what she meant. I've had older women proposition me before. It's flattering, I guess, but I wasn't interested in her. She's got a great body, but she's old."

"Yeah, probably nearing forty." He didn't seem to catch my attempt at humor.

"Did she think you'd refused her overtures because you were dating Emily?"

"I hinted at a girlfriend but I didn't say who it was. But she saw us around and after we broke up I guess I kind of cried on her shoulder once."

"So when she saw you two together, she might think you had made up—I mean you and Emily?"

"Yeah, I guess. She definitely saw us. She smiled at me but I guess she gave Emily what you might call a dirty look. But that was all and we left."

"Then what?"

"I drove her back to the sorority house and we talked for a few minutes in the car. We kissed goodnight and she went in."

"Did anybody see?"

"No. I stayed in the car on purpose. We thought it best if her sorority sisters didn't see us hanging out—at least not yet. Maybe somebody recognized my car that night, but I sure didn't see anybody. Is it important?"

"Really important. If we can prove that someone saw you drop Emily off at the house and drive away, that gives the police less reason to suspect you. You wouldn't be off the hook, but it would help."

"A while ago, you said 'we', Mr. Martindale. Does that mean you'll help me?"

"I'll do what I can."

And I would, but I still needed answers to a whole lot of questions.

"What do we do now?"

"I think you should turn yourself in, but I can't make you do it."

"I just can't do it! It puts a lie to all I've tried to make out of my life. I'll just be another black man in a lineup if I go to the police. I can't do it—yet. You've got to understand, I didn't do it!"

"It isn't my place to interfere. How long can you stay here?"

"Gabe's sister's going to be gone for a while."

He looked at Gabe who was standing in the door.

"That's cool," he said.

"Let's talk about coach and his wife. Emily seemed to think he treated his athletes badly."

"That's a bunch of shit!"

We both jumped at Gabriel Washington's loud voice. He was standing in the doorway looking particularly hulking, but seemed about to advance on me. Del shot me a look that told me to drop that particular subject for now. I would take the hint but I couldn't help wonder why Gabe was suddenly so worked up over this subject. But I wouldn't gain anything by antagonizing him now.

"Just a thought. I guess that really doesn't have anything to do with this. I really should be getting back to Corvallis."

I looked at my watch.

"It's almost eleven. I've got class tomorrow."

We stood up and shook hands.

"I'm in this thing with you. God knows why I get myself into things like this, but I do. I'll poke around and see what I can come up with. As far as I'm concerned, this whole evening never happened."

I looked over at Gabe.

"If word gets out that I'm helping you, my career is over or at best seriously compromised."

I turned back toward Del.

"He's cool, Mr. Martindale. He knows you're helping me. He just gets a little too hot under the collar for his own good sometimes. Right, Gabe?"

"Yeah. I intend to chill on this. I'm sorry I blew up. I just don't like it when people say bad things about coach or Mrs. M."

I met only a few cars on the way back to Corvallis and was in my condo shortly after midnight.

9

THURSDAY

got to campus early the next morning, feeling tired and cranky after my late night. I hadn't gotten to bed until well after midnight, then couldn't get to sleep as I thought about Del and Emily and my increasing involvement in something I should probably stay completely away from. I heard the phone as I put my key in the office door.

"Tom? Is that you?"

"In the flesh."

"It's Joel Friedkin, your friendly director."

"Yeah, Joel. Good morning. How are you?"

"Is what they say on the radio true? That black kid, Leroy . . ."

"Delroy."

"Yeah, yeah, whatever. Anyway, is it true the police are looking for him? They think he killed that girl, Amelia?"

"Emily. Emily Morgan."

"Yeah, yeah, whatever."

"So I hear. It's really a mess. I feel sorry for everybody concerned."

"Yeah, yeah. Too bad. But what do we do about our little ad series? The clock is running, Tom. Tragedy or not, we're into this now and we've got deadlines and air dates."

I almost said, "Yeah, yeah, whatever," but I refrained.

"We'll have to recast our leads."

"Pretty hard to deal with a corpse and a murderer. Heh, heh. Bad for the old image. Heh, heh."

"Look, Joel. Two lives are ruined here. It doesn't help things to have you making insensitive remarks."

"Yeah, yeah, whatever . . . But what do we do?"

I didn't answer as I sat massaging my forehead. I had felt a headache coming on as soon as I got up. The tenor of the day was only speeding up its arrival.

"Tom. Are you still there?"

"I'm here, trying to think what to do. Let me talk to my friend in theater arts. I'll get you some replacements who will be ready to go on Monday. That's when you're planning to come to campus, right?"

"That sounds like a plan. Call me if you have problems."

"See you Monday. Oh, Joel?"

"Yeah?"

"Has that Gates guy from the U of O been around any more?"

"Nobody's seen him. We're between shoots now so we've been all locked up. He couldn't get in if he tried. You find out anything about him from your end?"

"To tell you the truth, I haven't had time to check him out. I'll try to look into it later today. That's all I need right now—an industrial spy lurking around."

"Yeah, yeah, whatever."

"Say goodbye, Joel."

"Goodbye, Joel."

I hung up, wondering if I could stand much more of Joel Friedkin. I admired his skills as a filmmaker. It was his qualities as a person that worried me.

It was nearly time for class. I straightened my tie with the tiny scales of justice on it and grabbed my notes for a lecture on the law of libel. That kind of law wasn't what I was worried about.

| | |

"Libel is a defamatory statement about a person, a statement that is published, and as a result, injures that person's reputation. Reporters can get into trouble if their words imply criminality or question morals, sanity, or financial stability, or if mistakes are made in stating the facts of a story. For example, if you misspell a person's name or get their address wrong, it might be libelous. If a reporter, editor, and/or publication loses a suit for libel, they can be required to pay what are called damages."

I paused to write the word "damages" on the blackboard. I had begun by writing "libel" up there, too. I finished my lecture, interrupted here and there by questions.

"Now I'd like you to move your chairs around and split into five groups of five each. I guess one group will have to have six, if my quick count of you is correct. I want you to do a little exercise and then we'll get back together as a whole the last fifteen minutes of the period."

A mad scramble began, as students turned their desks into five rather irregular circles. The furniture squeaked as it was dragged across the floor. Friends sat with friends and shy kids actually spoke to their neighbors for the first time this term.

I had to shout to be heard over the clatter but they got quiet fairly fast.

"I've got five brief scenarios written on these sheets of paper, a different one for each group. Some are libelous, some are not. I want you to discuss the facts and then present an argument about whether the people in these cases were libeled or not. You can use your textbooks for reference if you want to. We'll get back together as a group in twenty minutes."

I have been turning away from straight lecture in recent years to group sessions as a way to reach this MTV generation of kids which wants you to put on a show, while they just sit in their seats waiting to be entertained.

I stepped out into the hall while they worked and walked to my office around the corner in the other wing. As I neared the fire doors cutting off the next section of the building, I saw someone standing at the door to my office. He seemed to be trying the door.

"Can I help you? Are you looking for me?"

The man turned and faced me, a somewhat startled and sheepish look on his face.

"Are you Tom Martindale?"

I nodded.

"Chuck Gates. I'm a . . . I work in the public affairs office at the U of O.

We shook hands.

"I've heard of you. Come in."

I unlocked the door and led him into my small conference room. I quickly slammed the door to my inner office, remembering that the storyboards and mock posters for the ad campaign were in plain sight inside.

"Sit down. I'd offer you coffee, but I'm in the middle of a class. The students are working in groups. I just ducked in . . . but you don't want to hear a treatise on my teaching techniques. What can I do for you?"

"I'm involved in the U of O ad campaign."

"May I congratulate you. Very impressive work."

"Thanks. We're pleased with it."

"Good results I'll bet."

"Our enrollment is way up."

"That's the general idea, I guess."

I wasn't about to gush all over Gates about the ads. They were outstanding—simple yet elegant images, a good narrator. I envied the budget he must have to buy time on what seemed to me to be all the right programs. Oregon University was so thrifty that I feared we'd complete our own ads, then find a general unwillingness to spend the $100,000 or so it would take to buy time on TV. The administration was willing to spend a fortune on a failing football program but not a campaign to increase enrollment.

"I was curious. I heard you were in charge of your university's ad effort and I thought we might get together . . . have lunch . . . or something—and maybe compare notes."

"I'm flattered that you've elevated my role here. I'm really just coordinating the work of other people. I wrote the script but . . . a lot of other people are involved."

Was this guy actually trying to get me to tell him the gist of our campaign? With the competition between our two schools almost unnaturally fierce at times, there was no way I would tell him anything. Besides, why would he care? They were winning this race very handily.

"Chuck. I've really got to get back to my class. They're probably rioting by this time."

I got up and steered him to the door and out into the hall.

"It's good to meet you. I have to be candid. I don't think anything would be served by me telling you what we're going to do."

Gates' manner suddenly changed.

"Do you think I'm trying to steal your ideas? Look, Tom. We're the University of Oregon! This place is . . . I'm just being honest here . . . a former cow college trying to pose as a university."

He had turned into a haughty bastard right before my eyes. What was this all about? I was mystified.

"I won't rise to your bait, Chuck. I could match you statistic for statistic on research dollars and facilities and excellence of teaching, but I haven't got time. It seems to me . . ."

I paused for effect and narrowed my eyes in what I hoped was a manner equal to his in the haughtiness department.

". . . that you wouldn't be skulking around in enemy territory like this if you weren't just a little worried about what we are planning to do."

"In your dreams, professor. I couldn't care less!"

He turned to leave.

"Oh, and one more thing, Chuck. Watch out for the cow dung as you walk to your car!"

10

"Duke Ramsay, please."

I was at my desk waiting for the head athletic academic adviser to come on the line.

"Hi, Duke. Tom Martindale in journalism. We served on that search committee together last year."

"Tom. Yeah, sure. I remember you. You're the guy who used to be that big time investigative reporter in New York."

"I'm not sure about the big time, but that's me. I'm calling to see if we can have lunch today. Excuse the short notice, but I figured we all have to eat and maybe you don't have plans."

"Yeah. Sounds good. I can make it. What time and where?"

"I'll pick you up at the side of the Coliseum at 11:45. We can beat the crowd at that place just north of downtown. If you like fish, that is."

"Love it, Tom. See you in . . . let's say thirty minutes."

"Bye."

Talking to Duke Ramsey would be a way to get some information fast. Before I left for lunch, I checked my e-mail. Five messages, none of them urgent.

Then I wrote out a brief account of my somewhat bizarre encounter with Chuck Gates for Hadley.

She was too busy to reach quickly on the phone, but I thought she ought to know what had happened. We had agreed to keep in touch electronically and sent messages back and forth every day. I finished my message:

So try to do some sleuthing around and find out what this guy is up to. Are they afraid of us or just curious? Let's talk in person soon.

Before I left my office, I took down all the posters and storyboards related to the ad campaign and locked them in a metal cabinet I had never locked before.

I I I

As with a lot of men who didn't like their given names, Ramsay hung onto his high school nickname. The university staff directory called him Roscoe but no one else ever did. A short, dark man with the build of a wrestler long since out of training, Ramsay was in charge of a section of the athletic department responsible for keeping student athletes eligible. In order to play, these kids had to maintain certain grade point averages. It was the job of Ramsay and his two assistants to make sure they did.

He was standing on the south side of the Coliseum, the Art Deco style building that housed the Department of Athletics. I leaned across the seat, unlocked the passenger door, and he got in.

"Right on time, Tom. How have you been?"

"It's not the best week of my life. Emily Morgan, the girl who got killed, was one of my students. I've really been upset over it."

"Yeah, I know what you mean. She worked in one of our tutorial programs. She was a great person."

"How's everything else, Duke?"

"Busy, very busy. Basketball season's in full swing."

I pulled out of the parking lot, turned right on 26th Street, then left on Western Boulevard for our drive to the restaurant, about ten minutes away.

"I suppose it's a problem keeping the basketball players eligible?"

"No, not at all. They're good kids, every one of them. It's the football players that give me fits. Those guys are in trouble all the time."

"Grade-wise, you mean."

"I mean . . ."

He looked around conspiratorially, before answering, as if he expected one of the big bruisers to materialize suddenly from the back seat.

". . . this is off the record, Tom, right?"

"I'm not going to write a story about our lunch conversation, Duke, if that's what you mean."

"Yeah, right. What I started to say is that football players get in all kinds of trouble—all kinds."

Just then I noticed a late model Corvette that I thought had been following us since we left campus.

"Do you know anyone who owns a Corvette, Duke?"

"Jesus! Is he following us? Won't they ever let me alone?"

"Who is it, Duke?"

He was looking increasingly agitated.

"Duke. Who is it?"

"Bobby Hardy, I think."

Bobby Hardy. Bobby Hardy. Why did that name seem familiar to me?

"A football player?"

"Yeah. A fullback and one of Coach Martino's favorites."

That was it. He was the player Del said had been with Mrs. Martino in the restaurant on the night Emily Morgan was murdered.

"How about Mrs. Martino? Is he one of her favorites too?"

"God, Tom. What do you know? God. Take me back to the Coliseum!"

"Take it easy, Duke. We haven't had lunch yet."

"Is the car still there?"

I glanced in the rearview mirror.

"Yeah, it's a couple of cars behind and there's two guys in it."

We went onto a short stretch of freeway, then stopped at a signal on Circle Boulevard, before turning right, crossing the railroad tracks and driving into the parking lot of the restaurant.

No sooner had we parked than the Corvette drove in next to us.

"Oh shit!"

Duke seemed really scared. I decided not to be intimidated by these thugs. In my best whistling-past-the-graveyard manner, I got out of the car.

The kid I took to be Hardy had parked next to my car on the passenger side. He was movie star good looking: well built and blond. The smirk on his face indicated that he was, as my grandmother used to say, stuck on himself. He opened the door.

"Help you out, Duke?"

He yanked hard on Duke's hand and the shorter man grimaced as he stood up.

"Hi, Bobby. Do you know Professor Martindale? From journalism? We're on this search committee together and we need to compare notes."

"How's it going?" I said. "Come on, Duke. I don't think Mr. Hardy is interested in why we're having lunch."

I started to walk toward the restaurant, but the other guy with Hardy in the car stood in my way.

"Bobby's not finished talking to you."

He was even bigger than Hardy, and a lot more menacing: a square blocky head, hair almost completely shaved, built like a large tree. He had a scar running from the corner of his left eye to his left ear.

"But I'm finished with him. I'm hungry."

I started to walk away, but he persisted in standing still. I kept going and was just ready to push him slightly when he stepped back.

"Shall we, Duke? These guys are late for class."

I turned around in time to see Hardy glaring at me, the first time he had dimmed his radiant, star athlete smile. He bent down and got very close to Duke's face.

"Have a nice lunch, Duke. Don't tell the professor here too many of our secrets."

He nodded at the scar guy and they both got back into the Corvette. I didn't look around as I heard him take at least a half-inch of rubber off his tires as he roared out of the parking lot. I opened the door for the pale-looking Duke and we walked in.

We both avoided talking about what had happened as we busied ourselves with looking at the menu and ordering. We were well into our French bread before either of us said anything.

"Do you know what that was all about? Why were they trying to intimidate us?"

"God. This couldn't be worse. They'll make my life miserable now."

"Who?"

He looked around to see if anyone was listening.

"Mrs. Martino."

He said the name in a loud stage whisper that probably was heard farther than he intended.

"The wife of the assistant coach?"

"Yeah."

"What's going on down there in the Coliseum? Make your life miserable in what way?"

"Oh God. I shouldn't be telling you this."

He was almost moaning from his fright.

"Duke. Calm down. Drink your water. Calm down. It'll help if you talk to me. Maybe I can help you if you tell me what you mean."

He gulped his water, choked in doing so, then coughed for several minutes as he tried to clear his throat.

"Are you all right, sir?"

The waiter was serving our meals.

"Yes, he's fine. He's got a sore throat. Thanks. This looks good. We'll call you if we need you." We both started to eat our meals, as soon as Duke stopped coughing.

"Okay, Duke. Go on. Tell me what you want to tell me. I think we've known one another long enough for you to trust me."

That, of course, was stretching things a lot. We had known one another for five years or so, but certainly not all that well. The forced intimacy of endless meetings of a search committee meant nothing more than time spent in a windowless room wishing we were someplace else. But maybe my feigned comradeship would lull him into talking.

"I need to get things off my chest. I've got to tell someone, so here goes."

He took a bite of fish for fortification and started to talk.

"Coach Brewster pretty much lets Ricky Martino run the team day-to-day. That's an open secret. He'll be retiring soon and a few alums really like him and want him to stay in place until he wants to leave. With Ricky running things, Coach Brewster can spend more time on his religious activities."

"On school time? At taxpayers' expense?"

"Not really," said Ramsay. "The athletic program uses public money for salaries. A lot of the budget for training comes from private sources. That's why these alums can have their way on a lot of things."

"Which alums?"

He glanced around again and lowered his voice even more.

"One is Darrel Granger. He owns a big timber company. The other is Elliot White, a stockbroker in Portland. They played football here in the glory days in the sixties."

"Interesting stuff, Duke. But you mentioned Martino's wife."

"Coach Martino lets his wife get involved with players more than a lot of us think is a good idea."

"Involved how?"

"Oh, she takes them out to dinner, maybe buys them things. There are even rumors that she lets them use some kind of vacation place she owns somewhere."

"So what's the problem? She's not on the staff and they're over eighteen."

"The problem is it doesn't look good when she lets them use it for recreation and spends time there herself."

"Just how does she define 'recreation'?"

Duke seemed genuinely frightened. Maybe he did have something to fear, although I couldn't be sure what that might be. In his mind anyway, he felt in danger.

"Duke. Listen to me. Calm down. You just keep out of anything involving the coach's wife. Don't tell me anything else."

We continued eating and eventually, Duke even ordered dessert.

"I'll have the deep dish apple pie a la mode," he said when the waiter returned. His fear hadn't diminished his appetite in the least. I declined, ordering a cup of coffee instead.

"Duke. Let's change the subject. I'm thinking about doing an article on athletes and the academic world."

I always hate myself when I lie so blatantly, but I plunged ahead all the same.

"An article?"

"You know I do teach journalism and write magazine articles and books whenever I get the time. I made my living as a writer before I came here to teach."

"Oh, yeah. We already talked about that."

Duke was happily wolfing down his pie a la mode, the fear of ten minutes before apparently gone.

"So what did you want to ask me?"

He wiped his mouth with a napkin and gazed contentedly.

"I wondered if you think student athletes are shortchanged when it comes to their studies? I'm not talking about the university here, I'm thinking student athletes in general."

"Do you mean do we exploit them for their skills on the playing field and ignore their need for a good education?"

"Yes. Exactly."

"Sometimes we do, yes. You didn't hear this from me, but all schools are guilty of that a little. I mean, it's my job to help these kids get their degrees."

"So what happens—I mean nationally, not just here. Mind if I take notes?"

A look of alarm flickered in his eyes, but he nodded.

"So you were going to tell me how this sad state of affairs happens."

"It happens because schools recruit kids more for their playing ability than anything else. In our case, we bring in a lot of minority kids from California who've had a tough time in school. Some of them can't read very well or write a complete sentence or even balance a checkbook. They belong in a community college somewhere, not a university."

"But we need them to win so we recruit them. But what happens when they get here and get into classes they aren't prepared for?"

"That's where my office comes in. We try to keep them eligible by making sure they don't flunk out. We pay for tutors for them. We contact professors on their behalf to see how they're doing."

"Do those contacts ever involve threats or bribes?"

"Not possible. The NCAA watches us like a hawk on all of this."

"NCAA?"

"The National Collegiate Athletic Association. It's the organization that controls college athletic programs. It makes the rules on everything and hands out the punishment."

"That may be true, but I have colleagues who have been pressured to pass someone who should be failing."

"Sometimes we point out what would happen to the team if a kid was flunked."

"So how do these kids usually do?"

Duke looked around the room before answering. "Less than half graduate."

"That's pretty sad," I said. "Do you ever think of the particular kid? I mean it does him no good to pass a course if it contains material he needs for the next course. He won't be prepared, so you've set up another possible failure. Cynics might say that this university—and a lot of other universities—recruit these kids knowing they are deficient academically. They recruit these kids to produce income for the school."

"I'm afraid I can't agree, Tom. Look at it another way. Our recruitment practices help youngsters from disadvantaged circumstances. We may not make university students out of these kids, but if we teach them to read and write, we've helped them improve their lives. They also make great contacts, I mean with people who help them later."

"Yeah, I suppose. But that doesn't change the fact that it's wrong to drop them like hot potatoes once they've used up their eligibility or ceased to play as well. The whole thing makes me mad. It is very unfair to them!"

"We take care of our guys."

Duke was sputtering out his excuses but they didn't sound convincing to me. I wondered if, in his heart of hearts, they were sounding all that convincing to him.

"We can argue this point forever and not agree. I know you're doing your best," I said, mostly to mollify him.

He nodded in agreement, a sad look on his face.

"Before we leave, I want to ask you about two black student athletes: Delroy Johnson and Gabriel Washington. How well do they do?"

"Del's a star. He's never been in a remedial program in his entire life as a student. He does well without even trying."

"And Gabriel?"

"Gabe's another story. He's had trouble with everything: reading, writing, math, history, even Black Studies. You name it, he's flunked it."

He stopped talking and turned red, suddenly realizing that he had just admitted the truth of what we had been talking about.

"Gabe exemplifies the kind of kid the system is harming the most."

He started to nod.

"You may have a point," he said grudgingly. "Gabe was in a program called Step-Up—to help him pass his courses. But he didn't do very well in that either."

He lowered his voice and contorted his neck to look again into the booth behind us. He was whispering again when he spoke.

"He's also not doing so hot on the playing field either. Rumors are that coach is dropping him from the lineup for next fall and stopping his financial support."

"Poor kid. Are he and Del friends?"

"Yeah, since grade school in south central L.A. Del tries to help him out, but he can't do it all for him. I just don't think Gabe's got much up here."

He tapped on his head.

"Did he have tutors?".

"Yeah, your student, Emily Morgan. She worked in that Step-Up program I mentioned."

"Horrible what happened to her. So she helped Gabe?"

Duke nodded and looked sad, and I didn't see anything else in his reaction. He didn't seem to know as much as I did about her death.

"Everyone in the offices around the department is really shaken up. The secretaries were crying all day yesterday, some of the players too."

"Same for us in journalism. Well, Duke, we'd better get back."

We each paid our share of the bill and headed for the door. I nodded and waved at several people I knew, but didn't stop to talk.

We didn't say much on the ride through town. It was a typical gray, cold winter day. Bare trees lined streets that were filled with early afternoon traffic.

"Duke. I want to ask you one last question."

He turned to me as we stopped at the traffic light on the street leading to the main entrance to campus.

"Is somebody trying to cover up a cheating scandal in the athletic department that would jeopardize NCAA eligibility for members of the team?"

A look of sheer horror crossed his face. He grabbed the handle and opened the door, even though traffic was beginning to move and I was easing my car forward. I stomped on the brakes hard.

"I'll get back on my own. I've been seen with you enough! I've told you too much already!"

11

As I walked in from the parking lot I began to think about how to find out more information about Mrs. Martino without raising the suspicion of the lady herself, her husband, or the kids who seemed to do whatever she asked. By the time I had reached my office, I knew precisely who to call.

I sat down at my desk and punched in the number I had memorized long ago.

"Jane. Hi, it's Tom Martindale."

"Tom. How are you? We haven't seen much of you lately."

Jane Quimby was the wife of my boss, the chairman of the Department of Journalism. The essence of style and grace, Jane was also a shrewd judge of people. She was well-connected in faculty wife circles. Faculty wives are the lower part of the iceberg that is the academic world—invisible but capable of sinking careers. Wives hold no position of authority, unless they hold campus jobs themselves. But faculty wives exert a great deal of influence in subtle, and not so subtle, ways. At the dinner table or during "pillow talk," wives comment on who to hire and fire, which faculty members are sleeping around, what powerful alumni think, and countless other details of daily life at a large university. Their husbands, whether president, provost, dean, or chairman, listen and sometimes act on this wifely advice—whether they admit it or not.

Jane wasn't interested in wielding power. She cared little about faculty wife intrigue and usually avoided social gatherings. She preferred devoting her time to raising her three children, caring for her husband, and keeping fit for her tennis game. She had been a champion player in college and still liked to play as often as possible. But she kept her political antennae extended enough to pick up information here and there.

"I know. I'm sorry. I pass your house a lot and I usually intend to stop but then I think I'd be interrupting you."

"Tom. You know that would never be true."

"What do you hear from Q?"

Lloyd Quimby, her husband and my boss, was on leave this term to gather material for a photography book he was writing.

"He's nearly finished at the Library of Congress and about to go up to that George Eastman museum in Rochester, New York."

Q's book is on the history of photography.

"Good. Glad it seems to be going well. I know he's having a good time. It's probably hog heaven for him to be able to immerse himself in all those old photos."

"I thought he had all the photos that ever were in our basement, but I guess the Library of Congress would even have him beat."

Q was notorious as a combination pack rat and junk man. He would never throw anything away if he thought he could use it or sell it. His basement contained everything from drawers of old type to several obsolete computers he kept for spare parts.

"Jane, I also called about something else, but not over the phone."

"Sounds mysterious and possibly scandalous. Just what I love to hear about," she replied, laughing.

"Could I drop by this afternoon?"

"I'll be waiting."

III

Fifty minutes later I was sitting in the Quimby's breakfast room, a bright, pleasant area off the kitchen where the family spent a lot of time. As we sat at the antique oak dining table and drank our Pepsis, two dogs slept at our feet and the screen of the television set danced with scenes of a volleyball game on the sand in Venice, California. The sound was muted but the colorful action seemed like a moving work of art, a match for the framed scenes of vintage athletic events arranged on the walls of the room.

"Now then, Tom. What's this all about?"

"I know I shouldn't begin a conversation with either you or Q by cautioning you about repeating what we say."

"But you're going to break that rule?"

"Yes. What I want to ask you about is serious stuff so I'd appreciate it if you keep it to yourself."

"Even Q?"

"Of course, you can tell him. I'd want him to be sitting here with us, if he was in town. But, don't mention it to him yet. I hope it will be all cleared up when he gets back."

"Not a word."

"Here goes. A student of ours was found dead two days ago."

"That girl in the dumpster behind the sorority? I guess I missed the fact that she was from the department."

I nodded.

"Poor thing. A beautiful girl, from her picture in the paper."

"A great girl—intelligent, gifted with a promising career ahead of her. The leading suspect is another student, not a J major. He's a black football player and the police are looking for him because he was the last person to see her alive. They used to go together but broke up. The police are trying to twist that into something unseemly."

"You don't think he did it?"

"No, I definitely do not. I've been sniffing around the edges here . . ."

"You've put your old investigative reporter's hat back on?"

"Well, yeah, I guess."

I felt my face grow red. She had caught me and guessed exactly what I planned to do.

"Don't be embarrassed, Tom. I think it's commendable, how much you care about your students. I really do—and so does Q."

"He does? Well . . . great!"

Lloyd Quimby was a person who never said much about what he felt. He let you know things indirectly, by vague grunts and raises of the eyebrow and the occasional pay raise and promotion.

"Anyway, my—I guess you'd call it sleuthing—has led me to suspect people other than my student, the football player."

I thought I wouldn't use any names with Jane.

"These people are in the athletic department or close to it. I'm not saying that any of these people killed the girl. I'd just like to know all I can before I get into this any more."

"And you think my old athletic network will help you?"

"That idea crossed my mind."

"You know I'll help you any way I can, but you've got to realize that my friends are not really in the power structure down there."

"I just thought you might hear something around the tennis court, something I could use."

"Well, sure, maybe. But it seems highly unlikely."

"There's another way you could help me more. Aren't you on the committee for the spring auction to raise money for summer camp for underprivileged children?"

"Yes. I don't mind listening to a little bit of prattle for a good cause."

"Is one of the committee members the wife of an assistant football coach?"

"Gloria Martino?"

"Yeah, that's who I mean. What do you think of her?"

"You want candor or sugarcoating?"

"Candor."

"I think she's a woman who spends too much time working on improving a body that still looks good, but not as good as she thinks it looks when she parades around trying to attract the attention of her husband's players."

"No, tell me what you really think, Jane."

She tilted her head back and laughed. "You said you wanted candor."

"Is it that obvious to a lot of people, or just to the more shrewd observers like you?"

"You mean the strutting around in front of players?"

I nodded.

"You bet. She wears clothes that are too tight. She shows a little too much cleavage. Her hair is a little too bleached. Her loop earrings are a little too big. Her tan is a little too dark, especially for Corvallis in the winter."

"Do they have kids?"

"The requisite blond boy and girl. Holy terrors, I've heard. They're on their own most of the time while mom is out . . . cavorting."

"Did you ever see her with football players—or talk to anyone who did?"

"Not personally, no. Do you know Carole Gardner?"

"Wife of the tennis coach?"

"Yes. Carole and I are old friends. Carole told me once that she saw Gloria one night in the pool in the men's gym swimming with two hunky young men and none of them had on a stitch of clothing—not even a Speedo or a bikini."

"Amazing."

"You bet. And I remember Carole observing that Gloria Martino didn't seem to care who saw them. Can you beat that? How brazen!"

"Gloria Martino sounds like quite a piece of work."

"Does any of this fit with what you already know? And how does it tie in with that poor girl's murder?

"I'm not sure. I haven't found a connection, but I'm still looking."

"You don't think Gloria had something to do with killing that girl? I can't imagine anything as bad as that. Gloria's many things but I don't think she's a murderer."

"I doubt it, too, but I wonder if the team is somehow involved. The girl was a tutor for players, so she was known around the athletic department. I don't know much, but the whole thing doesn't seem right to me. I'm still putting it together."

"When you do, let me know."

I looked at my watch.

"It's late. I've got to get back to campus and grade some exams."

12

My office is a good place to work, especially at night when no one is around. I went back there after eating to grade the exams for my history seminar and to finish plans for the ad shoot, which would begin on campus on Monday.

I kept eyeing the pile of twenty blue books, exams waiting to be corrected.

"No, Melissa. Two early government restrictions on press freedom were not the Alien and *Seduction* Acts!" I laughed as I docked this hapless young woman seven points with my red pen.

I shook my head and put down my pen. I counted the number of exams remaining. I often did this in an effort to gain confidence that I was almost through. It was hard to concentrate. I couldn't help thinking about Emily, Del, and the mysterious Gloria Martino.

After five minutes or so of such musings, I forced myself to finish. All of that took about forty-five minutes. I looked at my watch: 11:15. I took off my glasses and rubbed my forehead.

"Whew! Long day."

I leaned back in my chair, spread my arms and stretched. It was time to go home. I placed the stack of exams on a side shelf and walked toward the door, picking up my coat and overcoat. I turned off the lights and closed and locked the hall door.

My car was parked in the lot just south of the building. As I unlocked it, I heard giggling coming from a couple who had come around the side of the men's gym down the street and were stopped at the door, fumbling with a key.

I eased over to the edge of the lot and strained to see what was going on. I could tell what they were doing because of the strong light above the door, but they couldn't see me because of the hedge growing all around the parking lot.

Eventually, the woman got the door unlocked. As the man grabbed the handle and stepped back to hold the door open for her, he was illuminated by the light.

"I'll be damned! Bobby Hardy."

I didn't need three guesses to figure out who his companion was. It had to be the infamous Gloria Martino. Were they about to go skinny-dipping in the university pool? Issues of voyeurism aside, I was really curious.

I waited for them to get involved in whatever it was they were going to get involved with before I walked across the street to try to open the door myself. Sometimes these old doors didn't quite click if they weren't slammed. These two had closed the door slowly to deaden the sound. Just maybe . . .

I held my breath and tried it. Bingo.

I opened the door slowly and ducked inside. The smell of chlorine overwhelmed my nostrils as soon as I stepped in the door. The pool—and the nocturnal swimmers—were not far away. I'd need to be careful and quiet.

I was in a small lobby with doors at either end leading to both the pool area and locker rooms. If my memory wasn't failing me, a stairway at the other end led to a gallery at the top of the building where spectators watched swim meets. That would be a perfect vantage point for me now. I hurried across the lobby and crept up the stairs, pausing every second or so to listen.

As I reached the top, I heard the same giggling that attracted my attention earlier. I eased through a partly open door and was immediately aware of a stronger chlorine smell and the kaleidoscope of images the rippling water was making on the ceiling.

"Okay handsome. What do you think of me now?"

Gloria Martino was standing on the side of the pool wearing a short robe, which she opened. Even after two kids, she was attractive. Her body was firm and well-proportioned.

As she said that, Hardy swam to the edge of the pool right below her and looked up.

"Oh boy, have I died and gone to heaven or what?"

She laughed and sat down on the edge of the pool. He started rubbing her legs and soon reached up to pull her into the water with him. I was sure he had left his bathing suit in the locker room too. They kissed and fondled each other as they twisted and turned in the water. Before long, they were involved in a more heated sport, amid a lot of moaning and splashing water,

They swam toward my end of the pool on their backs. Her long blond hair floated in the water around her head and, yep, he had left his bathing suit somewhere else. When they got to a point below where I was hiding, the two of them stopped to tread water.

"God, what a rush! I love doing it to you in the water, Gloria. How about on the floor, or on a bed sometime?"

"Don't call me Gloria."

"All right, all right, Mrs. M," he said.

"If you talk dirty to me, I won't be able to be with you again. And I won't let you help me solve my problems."

"Gloria, God no! Don't even say that. I want you. I need you. You're all I think about! I'll do anything you want me to"

Then I heard more splashing water and moaning.

"Easy, Bobby, you little stud."

She laughed and the water splashed some more. Just then I got a cramp in one foot and shifted my weight slightly. The floor gave out a distinct squeak which echoed loudly in the quiet building.

"What was that? Did you hear anything?"

Mrs. M was jumpy, as well she might be.

"Who's up there? Is somebody there? It'll be best if you come on out. If I have to come after you, you won't like what I do to your face."

Yeah, right. Like I'm going to come out with my hands in the air. This kid was fast, however, and seemed to know the building. Before I knew it, he was out of the water and heading toward the lobby. From there he could easily block my exit down the stairs.

What to do? I slipped along the railing on my hands and knees to the far end of the balcony.

"Bobby, someone's moving around up there."

Gloria Martino was just below me, still in the water.

Several years before I had been a member of the facilities and planning committee charged with overseeing building maintenance. At one point during my three years on the committee, the roof of this building had partially collapsed after an ice-covered tree had fallen on it. We had toured the building and I remembered a fire exit up here somewhere.

I reached the end of the balcony and paused to look up.

"Where are you, you son of a bitch? You're going to be sorry if I have to come up there to find out."

Bobby Hardy was waiting in the lobby, so certain was he that he could block the only exit from the balcony.

Almost hidden in the wall was a small opening about the size of a kitchen cabinet door. I opened it carefully and looked in. It was totally black inside. I felt around for a foothold and found the top rung of a ladder.

"Okay, you bastard! I'm coming up. I warned you."

I could hear Hardy's bare feet slapping each step as he made his way up the stairs in an exaggerated manner designed to scare me. I grabbed the rung and hoisted myself through the tiny door, pulling it shut when I was safely inside.

The chlorine smell was stronger in here and it was also a lot warmer than in the cavernous pool area I had just departed. I started climbing down the ladder slowly, feeling my way lest I slip and fall into whatever lay below.

Hardy's threats were hard to hear now. The walls of this vertical passageway were thick. The farther down I climbed, the more aware I became of the sound of a large machine. A few feet more and I could see light below me and hear what sounded like hissing. Then, it dawned on me. I was about to enter the maintenance tunnel for the steam heating system still used in many of the older buildings on campus.

Although the light was dim in the area where I stepped down from the ladder, I could see where I was. I was standing in what looked like a short spur leading into the main tunnel. I knew from my previous guided tour that the steam tunnel ran east and west parallel to the main street leading into campus, with a branch heading north.

I had wondered for years why the sidewalks leading to my building were free of snow, even in the worst storms. The answer, of course, was that steam from the tunnels below heated the cement above.

I headed toward the light in the main tunnel. I couldn't see the source of the hissing but I decided right away that I needed to keep away from the menacing hot pipes running along the walls on both sides. I put one hand up to the nearest pipe and quickly pulled it back for fear of getting burned.

The tunnel would be a good route of escape if I kept to the center and didn't scald myself. Every so often, I paused to listen for him crashing along after me. At first, I heard nothing. Soon, however, an unmistakable sound reached my ears.

"Son of a bitch! Ow. That hurts . . . Gloria, throw me my clothes!"

Hardy was still in the altogether. I would gain time while he waited for some clothes. I hurried along the tunnel where it branched off toward the north, but decided to keep going down the hill. I wanted to get as far away as possible from him. I could double back for my car later.

As I reached a point just beyond the junction, I saw what looked like yellow lights shining towards me. Then, the lights moved. I stopped and waited to allow my eyes to adjust to the dim light.

After a moment or two, I saw three creatures on a ledge ahead of me. They jumped down and waddled toward me, curious about this interloper intruding on their private domain. They sniffed my shoes and I stood still.

Rats? Mice? No, this had to be a trio of nutria, rodent-like creatures introduced to Oregon in the 1950s in a plan to raise them for their fur. The scheme had not worked out and many of the little devils had been released into the wild by investors trying to forget they had ever gotten involved in this caper.

I had long heard rumors that some were living in these tunnels and elsewhere in the dark recesses of campus. Here was the proof.

They were apparently harmless, but I didn't want to risk being bitten. I remained still until they were behind me, then I picked up the pace.

Suddenly, it dawned on me. Bobby Hardy might not be as benign in his reaction. I stopped and turned around to listen.

I didn't have long to wait. In several minutes, I could hear him come crashing along the tunnel.

"Okay, you bastard. I'm going to catch you. And when I do . . ."

I waited and kept listening.

"What the hell! Oh God! Rats! Gloria. There's rats down here! Oh God!"

He was screaming in real terror. Why didn't he just run away? Then I heard him fall.

"Get away from me, you little bastards! Get away!"

He was apparently trying to get up but probably kept tripping over his own feet when he did so.

"Owww! Ooohhh! No! Ouch! That hurts!"

I didn't think he was being attacked by the nutria. They weren't hostile, only curious. But after how he had behaved, I certainly wasn't going to come to his rescue.

"That's hot! Ouch! Oh no!"

Then I heard a thud and a loud rumbling noise that reverberated through the pipes alongside where I was standing. Hardy had apparently fallen against the hot steam pipes and had burned himself in the process.

"Gloria. I'm burning up! Help me! Oh God!"

I raced along the tunnel toward the next lighted area. I would be in front of Snell Hall by this time. I walked into a branch heading into that building and soon came to a grillwork. I edged toward it and looked out.

If I removed this covering and stepped through, I would be in the loading dock area of the building. I kicked the grill with one foot. It remained in place. I paused, then kicked again. This time, the old screws holding the grill gave way and it broke free, dropping with a clatter to the floor on the other side.

I waited, listening for the sound of a security guard whose attention could have been attracted by the sound. No one came so I climbed down. I stood the grill back up along the wall and walked quickly out the door into the cold night.

I still had to get back to my car and to report Bobby Hardy's presence in the tunnel. I walked through campus as fast as I could to Monroe Street, an area of stores adjacent to campus. There I found a pay phone to call campus security.

"There's a man in the steam tunnel under the men's gym."

Then I hung up. I walked leisurely back to my building. I waited just inside the door for the police.

As I stood there, I saw a blond in a fur coat run through an opening in the hedge. Gloria Martino. I had to get a better look. I walked quickly outside and went directly to where she was frantically trying to unlock the door of a low-slung red sports car.

"Excuse me, ma'am. Do you need some help?"

Mr. Good Samaritan.

"Oh God, you scared me." She looked frightened and put her hand over her heart as if to quiet its rapid beating. Then, she dropped her car keys.

"Sorry. I was working late in my office." I motioned vaguely toward the building behind me, then picked up her keys.

"The campus is pretty safe, but at this hour, you never know."

My reassuring tone seemed to calm her and she smiled. Gloria Martino was beautiful even if in a somewhat brassy, overdone way. I felt a certain excitement even in talking to her. It was easy to see why these college guys would go over the top.

I unlocked the door and she slid behind the steering wheel, her coat rising slightly to reveal a shapely and tanned bare leg as she did so. She could make a man forget his problems—whatever they were. I handed her the keys and she turned on the ignition.

"Thanks a lot. I appreciate your help. I did feel a bit panicky before. I'm lucky you came along."

"My pleasure."

She gave me a big smile before backing out. She stopped before driving away and rolled down the window. I leaned in closer.

"I don't even know your name."

"Tom Ma . . . Tom." No last names under the circumstances.

"Mr. Tom, thanks again," she said with a big smile. Blanche Dubois could not have said it better.

As she rolled up the window, I caught a whiff of the kind of perfume ads say will send men reeling. How had she managed to smell that good, straight out of the pool?

13

FRIDAY

The next morning after class, my curiosity got the best of me so I called Lieutenant Pride. She picked up her own phone on the first ring.

"Angela Pride, State Police."

"Tom Martindale, Angela. How are you?"

"Tom Martindale, ace sleuth and reporter? Tilter at lost windmills?" All of that was pretty jaunty for Angela.

"Sorry to bother you on this gloomy Friday but I was just wondering if you knew any more about the murder of Emily Morgan."

"Not much more than two days ago. We've taken a lot of statements from her sorority sisters and classmates. Her father is arranging for the body to be taken back to Medford tomorrow, I think. We've been waiting on the autopsy results from the coroner. I just got a copy."

"And?"

"You know I can't discuss it, Tom. It'll be used in the trial when we catch the guy who killed her."

"So you think it's a guy, Angela?"

"All right. What I'm going to tell you is just between us. Will you swear to keep this quiet? I mean no one is to know this. Do you agree?"

"Of course. I'm only asking for my own knowledge.

"I'll say this once only. Emily Morgan was pregnant when she died."

Suddenly, I felt sick to my stomach. I bit the back of my hand to hold back the tears forming in my eyes.

"So you think the guy who made her pregnant also killed her?"

"No, I don't know that the killer and the man who made her pregnant are one in the same. She was not raped, if that is what you are getting at. She died from hitting—or being hit over—her head."

"But it is a logical conclusion that it's the same guy. Right? Otherwise it makes no sense."

"Murderers aren't always logical, Tom. They're nuts. But you're right. She might have been killed by someone really in a rage. He might also be getting rid of evidence that he made her pregnant."

"So you have no doubt that the killer is a man?"

"Probably, but we're not ruling out anyone. Including you."

"What?"

"Don't worry. But I'm going to charge you with something if you don't get your academic ass over here and give your statement."

"I know, I know. Could I wait until next week? I'm in the middle of having the camera crew on campus for that ad shoot I told you about. I have a really hectic week ahead."

"Yeah, I guess. I know you're not going anywhere. But I need to talk to you because what you told me before implicates that football player, Delroy Johnson."

"Yeah, I know. I hate that I got him in trouble like that."

"You were just telling me what happened. If you'd held out on me, I'd have gotten you for obstructing justice."

I gulped and changed the subject. If Emily was pregnant, Del was probably the father and that gave him a very strong motive to kill her.

"Speaking of Johnson, Angela. Have you located him yet?"

"No sign of him. He's just vanished. We talked to most of the team members, but not Johnson. Speaking of which: a real odd thing happened to one of his teammates last night."

"Oh, what was that?"

"This kid . . . let's see, his name is in my report here. Robert James Hardy. We found him dressed only in Speedo trunks huddled in one of the steam tunnels near the men's gym. He was raving about big rats chasing him. He was crying and his butt was burned. He was calling for someone named Gloria. Real strange."

"Oh, poor kid. Must be the pressure of mid-terms or something."

14

That afternoon, I had to make a presentation to the University Image Enhancement Committee. Even though I was doing all of the campus staff work on the ad campaign under Hadley Collins' direction, I had to go through the motions of reporting on my activities to the committee that was nominally in charge. In return, I would get the benefit of members' "counsel and guidance."

The basic idea of the committee system—here and probably every other college in the country—is to bring people together from all parts of the university to carry out some assigned task, whether it be decisions on promotion and tenure or seeing that animal research was conducted humanely.

The reality, however, is often quite different. As a committee member, you are forced to sit through endless meetings while members who never do much real work pontificate on whatever subject the committee is supposed to be concerned with. Moreover, it often seems that the system is designed to deflect all blame and responsibility from administrators hired and paid well to make the really tough decisions.

This was what I feared would be happening this afternoon in the rather pompous sounding Image Enhancement Committee. In business, you'd call it the marketing committee or the public affairs committee, using words with a clear meaning to describe such important work. But not in the academic world, where words are used to camouflage things, to sound erudite just for the sake of sounding erudite.

Some committees have real power and a reason for existence. Others are anachronisms that should have been put out of their misery a long time ago. In most committees, the chairman and one or two members do all of the work. The others merely attend meetings. But all have equal power. This means that someone who has never done a lick of work for a committee can come to a meeting and sabotage the efforts of the few who have done everything. This was pretty much the case here: I was doing all the work but had to give members the chance to pick it apart.

We were to convene at three thirty in the president's conference room. As soon as I got there I set up an easel in the front to display storyboards for the TV spots and several of the print ads we intended to run in newspapers around the state. I finished my preparations as Hadley walked into the room.

"Hi, Tom. Good to see you. Is it reverse sexism to say how distinguished you look in that pinstriped suit? And that tie—what's on it?"

She leaned forward so close that I could smell her perfume.

"Hot air balloons?"

"What else, given the purpose of this committee?"

She started laughing and shaking her head. "I like your sense of humor, Tom."

"Thanks. Most of the time it's too subtle for a crowd like this."

"Before everybody else gets here, I wanted to ask if you'd heard any more from our U of O spy?"

"I haven't had the time to pursue it further."

"I wouldn't bring it up today." She looked around conspiratorially and lowered her voice. "That would be all that some people need to derail things this afternoon. Nothing would be served by your mentioning it, I don't think."

"I agree. It could easily turn into a major diversion. I'd like to get through this quickly so I can get ready for more shooting next week."

"Edna. How are you?"

We both turned as a tall, rather stout woman in a flowing cape came sweeping through the door. Edna Blandings Conway was an associate dean of home economics and a formidable figure on campus for thirty-five years. She had solid credentials for this committee, having served in the marketing department of Sears before joining the faculty. She also had another requirement for service in home economics: three names. Everyone I've ever known from there, married or single, always has three names.

She extended her hand which I took and shook gently. I simultaneously stepped around to help remove her cape in an attempt at gallantry. Unfortunately, in the process, I caught my finger in her brooch, cutting it slightly. In an effort to keep my blood from staining the velvet of her cape, I allowed it to fall to the floor. Then, to make matters worse, I stepped on the garment, stumbling against her slightly in the process. She recoiled at my touch and I leaped back quickly.

"Sorry, Dean Conway. I'm all thumbs today."

She glared at me and bent down to pick up her then slightly bedraggled looking cape.

"It's all right! I'll get it!

Was there an edge to her voice? I couldn't be sure, but she was practically shouting.

Another loud voice began competing with Dean Conway's.

"Good day, everyone."

Carson Bradshaw, a business professor, stepped through the door. Like many people who are losing their hearing, Bradshaw usually shouted. When I talked to him I always thought of that old "Saturday Night Live" news routine in which the "closed captioning for the hearing impaired" involved someone shouting from the bottom of the screen.

The three of us smiled and nodded simultaneously as he settled his tweed-attired figure in the chair opposite mine.

A small, thin, rather pale woman came in next: Liz Stein, a political scientist. She always dressed like someone about to join the Contras in Nicaragua or the Shining Path in Peru—or whatever guerrilla band was in fashion now. She wore a blue work shirt, faded jeans, and a bright red bandanna on her head. Every time I saw her, I wondered what revolutionary group the small eagle's head tattooed on her neck represented. Probably seeing it too, Edna Blandings Conway looked appalled, but managed to smile weakly as Liz sat next to her.

"Hi, Liz. Good to see you." I reached across and shook her hand. But that wasn't an easy thing to do because she turned it into some kind of revolutionary high five. Edna Blandings Conway was not amused at this either.

"Read any good books or written any good sentences lately, Martindale?" a voice said behind me.

"Don't tell me. Let me guess. It's my esteemed colleague from the Department of English, Edd Wells, that's 'Edd' with two 'Ds'."

Our banter obscured long-standing friction between us. We joined the faculty the same year and have known each other for over ten years. Beyond our basic disagreement over what constituted good writing, we had always been rivals in our climb up through the ranks. Even though Edd worked in a separate department and was subject to different criteria than I, he hadn't been promoted to full professor as I had five years before. That meant that, although he had tenure, he would probably remain an associate professor for the remainder of his career. Rank means more in academe than in the world outside our hallowed halls. Ascendancy is slow and careful and, as a result, means more when you get the perks that go with it, like a title.

Wells would be one of the perpetual associates and he somehow blamed me for it. He vented his anger and frustration on me by being very, very picky. I didn't really fear what he would say, I just dreaded all the time he would take to say it.

He sat down next to me, a fact I hated because he had the annoying habit of constantly reading whatever paper I had in front of me. On other committees I've even had him propose ideas I had jotted down before it was my turn to speak.

"Sorry. Hope I'm not late."

Margaret Rollins came in next. She was the newly named chairwoman of the Department of Speech and Theatre. No one knew how she felt about the university's image or much of anything else. She had only recently joined the faculty and our committee. I liked her right away because of her ability to camouflage a no-bullshit attitude beneath the soft drawl of her native Mississippi.

She was attractive and very well dressed. Edna Blandings Conway nodded her approval. Liz Stein looked more revolutionary than ever in comparison.

"I'll have to leave early. I'm booked for two other meetings today."

Webster "Skip" Olson, director of alumni, had arrived. A reasonably nice guy, Skip always spent a lot of time telling everyone how busy he was. He had the infuriating habit of bringing his cell phone into the meeting. He also seemed to relate everything to some alum or other, living or dead. He could rattle off who was married to whom and the year they graduated. Unfortunately, that information wasn't always relevant to whatever was being discussed.

For a large man—easily six foot five inches, with a generous amount of weight on his immaculately clad body—Olson moved quite quickly. In fact, he worked the room like a politician, walking around the large table to shake hands and have a personal word with everyone present. He eventually made his way around to me and sat on my left.

"Tom. Saw some old students of yours at the winter retreat last weekend."

"Those in their seventies or what?"

He looked puzzled, then got my feeble joke.

"Oh, Tom. You'd be a hundred to have students in their seventies. You're in remarkable shape, but not that well-preserved."

He dug his elbow into my rib and laughed cheerfully.

"I should have said your former students. You writers are such sticklers for precision in language."

"A journalist is not a writer and not very precise about anything," Edd chimed in from my other side. I ignored him.

"Who did you see, Skip?"

"Let's see, I have his card here in my case. He paused to put on his glasses and then squinted at the small type.

"Steve Mallon, class of 1989, and his lovely wife Melanie Whiting Mallon, class of 1990. He's an editor at *The Oregonian*. She's in marketing at some high tech company. They both spoke highly of you as a teacher."

My God. He even knows the wife's maiden name. "Good. Nice to hear. I remember them both. It's very rewarding to see your students do well and think that you might have played a small part in their success. That's the great thing about journalism training, Skip. It prepares you for a meaningful career."

Skip was nodding agreeably, but Wells started muttering. "God damn trade school stuff."

I kept ignoring him.

"I think we need to begin. I am convening the fourth meeting of the University Image Enhancement Committee at three thirty-three p.m." Hadley Collins used her voice as a gavel and everyone else at the table immediately quieted down. Almost as one, the members of the committee turned on their Palm Pilots as if they were a weapon in battle. I first became aware of this peculiar product several years ago when I noted in the staff newsletter a class on how to "maximize your utilization of your PDA system."

I have refused all suggestions to buy a Palm Pilot or other PDA device. I know I could use it to organize my day, my week, even my year electronically. I could keep names and addresses in there, even interview notes. I have resisted for one simple reason. It's so much simpler to use my pathetic little pocket calendar. I take a kind of perverse delight in attending meetings with it sitting on the table in front of me. It is really amusing to see fellow members of this or other committees gravely consulting their PDAs.

"I hope we won't be here beyond five," said Edd Wells.

Fat chance. Everyone always get restless at five o'clock and begins to pack up in the same way students do if your lecture runs even a minute over the end of the period.

"This is probably as good a time as any to talk about our next meeting," said Skip Olson, beginning the usual litany of members about how busy they are. On any meeting of any committee I'd ever attended, the toughest thing was not dealing with whatever subject we were there to handle, but finding a convenient time to meet. "I'm out for the next two weeks. Going with the president on a West Coast swing to visit alumni groups in the Bay Area and southern California."

Why is it that university officials always schedule their "swings" to visit alumni and prospective student in sunny California during Oregon's rainy season? I wonder.

"I'm in New York for the fashion previews week after next," said Edna Blandings Conway.

"Why are we looking at our calendars?" As usual, Carson Bradshaw was hopelessly lost.

"Three weeks from today is the winter socialist political action seminar in Berkeley," said Liz Stein. She was smiling slightly, no doubt contemplating those sessions on barricade storming and eye-cleansing-after-tear-gas.

"Look, people. We could spend the next hour setting up our next meeting, but I didn't call us together to do that." Hadley Collins was looking more than a little annoyed. "I convened this committee so that Professor Martindale could bring us up to date on the advertising campaign he is ably—how should I put it—co-directing?"

I nodded and glanced around the table. Everyone looked up from their Palm Pilots. Edna Blandings Conway was smiling, but frowned as she fingered the brooch on her dress. I hoped the fragments of my blood would flick off in time.

Liz Stein smiled too and gave me some kind of clenched fist salute. Carson Bradshaw did a modified "hip, hip, hooray" yell and raised a finger and thumb to form the "O" that generally means "okay." I'm told that in Italy it means something just the opposite and making the gesture can get you slapped or punched.

Margaret Rollins smiled and perpetual freshman Skip Olson on my left patted me on the back and tried to raise my arm in a kind of victory salute. On my other side, however, my colleague in the world of the written word, Edd—with two Ds—Wells, was very quiet while this spontaneous display of affection toward me was going on.

"We are all grateful to you Tom, for taking this on, on top of what I know is your heavy class load in the journalism department and on-going writing projects," said Collins. "Why don't you fill us in on where things stand?"

I stood and walked to the front of the room, a folder containing my notes tucked under one arm. I placed it on the table along with my watch and turned to face the committee.

"Thank you, Vice-president Collins. As many of you know, this project—and the university as a whole—experienced a real tragedy earlier this week when

Emily Morgan, one of the lead participants in our advertisements, was found, apparently murdered, in the alley behind her sorority house. Emily was a student of mine. She had been my advisee since her freshman year. I'd like us at this time to stand for a moment of silence in her memory."

I looked around and everyone but my nemesis from English, Edd Wells, was beginning to rise.

"This is ridiculous," he muttered in a kind of stage whisper that everyone probably heard. He only joined the others in standing after Edna Blandings Conway gave him a particularly dirty look.

I let the second hand on my watch move past one minute before speaking again. "Thank you. I know Emily's family will appreciate this gesture. The sadness of our loss cannot transcend the need to meet the deadline of the production company. If we want to get these ads on television by spring, we will have to stick to our schedule. Emily's death puts us even more behind because we'll have to re-shoot the scenes she did earlier this week in Portland. Let's talk about the script. All of you have copies. I . . ."

"Shall I tell you about your faulty parallelisms?" interrupted Wells. It was so like Edd to try to turn even an advertising script into something written as an arcane paper to be presented to the Modern Language Association.

"And what's this 'our' stuff? I wasn't aware of a vote taken on any of this." Wells was muttering just loud enough for only those sitting near him—and me—to hear.

"Professor Wells, please," said Hadley. "There will be plenty of time for questions later. Tom's task is hard enough without having to put up with second guessing from the rest of us."

She was smiling but her message was clear: shut up and back off. He nodded but glared at both of us.

"As I was saying, our aim in these ads is to interest high school students in attending the university by showing them the variety of majors available here. To do that, we'll use attractive students filmed on campus and in the Portland studio of the filmmaker doing the actual production work.

"We've put together focus groups in the Portland area and eastern and southern Oregon. This means we've tested the concept with the kind of high school students we want to attract here."

I finished my presentation in twenty minutes and stopped for questions, walking back to my chair.

"How were the student actors selected?" Margaret Rollins asked.

"I consulted with Kate Mason, your colleague in drama, and also used my own contacts with students who look good and I thought could do this."

"So now you're a casting coach as well as an ad man," Wells muttered.

"Professor Wells. Did you have something to say?" said Hadley Collins. "I couldn't quite hear you."

"Err, I wondered how this compares with what the University of Oregon is doing? They've been running a good advertising campaign for years."

Good save, Edd, but I'm sure she heard what you really said.

"I agree, Edd," I added cheerfully. Even if this jerk was trying to trip me up, he was right this time.

"The U of O has great ads, but I don't think we want to copy them or even think about them as we do this project. We need to do something entirely different—not only as good, but better in a different way."

"Fat chance with you in charge." Edd was not going to give up. I ignored him for now.

"We'll wipe up the floor with the U of O!" Carson Bradshaw shouted, this time pounding the air with his outstretched arm, his hand making a fist.

We all laughed at his spontaneous outburst.

"And what about the football player, the other lead?" Wells had better sources of information on campus than I would have given him credit for.

"Right, Edd. Glad you brought him up. Delroy Johnson, a football player and excellent student . . ."

". . . of literature . . ."

Edd was having no trouble in the running dialogue department today.

"Johnson is in the ads too and we may have to re-cast him," I said.

"He's on the run, Tom. Isn't that it?" continued Wells. "The police are looking for him so they can question him about the Morgan girl's murder."

Edna Blandings Conway gasped. Feminist/political scientist Liz Stein tried to comfort her but she kept pulling away.

I looked directly at Edd as I continued my report.

"I'm not altogether clear on Delroy Johnson's status with the police. What I do know is that, because of the circumstances, I've decided to get another student to read those lines and appear on camera."

"Maybe not a black guy this time, Tom. Okay?"

Alumni Director Skip Olson looked like he hadn't intended to utter the words that just left his mouth, but was not, at the same time, sorry he said them.

"You've got something against black people, Skip?" Liz Stein's face had turned crimson and she was glaring across the table at the now sheepish looking alumni director. I felt it was a good thing the table was wide or she might have leaped over it and grabbed him by the throat.

"Oh no. It's not that. I'm not a racist."

"I really don't know you at all," Liz continued, obviously very angry. "If you have to say you're not whatever it is, then it may mean you have tendencies to be just that." Liz was unbowed, but Skip persisted. I decided to keep quiet.

"It's just that some of the older alumni don't like it when the face we present to the world is that of a black guy and a white girl. They might threaten to withhold some contributions."

I could not believe what I was hearing. A university of our standing having people like this in positions of power! Now I was the one who was appalled. No wonder Emily and Del had encountered problems.

"How did they know what we were doing?" I asked, trying to control my growing anger. "Our plans were supposed to be kept confidential. I thought it was understood that everything we cover in these meetings and any written material I give you are not for distribution or outside discussion."

"Well, I showed it to some members of our executive committee." Skip was sputtering out his answers and turning red in the face.

"And the script didn't say that one of the principals in the production would be black."

Now I was sputtering.

"I . . . I sort of told them. . . I mean who it was. They knew Del Johnson and . . ."

"So it's okay to have a black kid win football games for you but not a good thing to let him onto the television screen," I said.

Carson Bradshaw was on his feet and pointing a finger at Skip Olson, his tone of voice Shakespearean.

"This man is a traitor to his profession!"

I raised both hands as speech professor Margaret Rollins coaxed the old man back into his chair.

"Please everybody, we've got to keep calm. This is getting out of hand. We all seem to be a bit on edge today. Under the circumstances, maybe I should save my longer presentation until another day."

I looked at the vice-president who was nodding her approval.

"Let me pass out a revised script which also details my plans to replace the two students. Please read this and contact me over the weekend if you have any problems with my plans."

I walked around the room myself and looked everyone in the eye. They were beginning to turn off their PDAs, a sure sign that we were winding down.

"I can't emphasize enough the importance of keeping this confidential. We want our ads to be a surprise and we don't want that school with the big green O to know what we're doing."

They all smiled at my lame attempt at humor, except Edd, who was looking out the window at some distant point in the sky.

We quickly dispersed. I promised to call the vice-president over the weekend to hash this over. As always with executives at her level, she had another meeting.

The others were milling around the elevators so I took the stairs. I was tired of all of them and didn't particularly want to spend any more time with them just then.

I reached the outside of the building before they did and started walking up the hill to the safety of my office. I was aware of someone walking up to me from the front of the field house before I actually saw who it was.

"Hi, Gabe. I'm surprised to see you."

It was Gabriel Washington, Del Johnson's good friend.

"What's going on?"

We were heading toward a group of faculty people walking down the hill, probably to another meeting. I nodded to them.

"Hi, Sue. Hello George."

While they were still within earshot, Gabe spoke in a louder than normal voice.

"I wanted to return this book. Thank you for letting me borrow it."

Saying that, he darted away from me and down the street toward the baseball field.

Although we both knew that Gabriel hadn't ever borrowed a book from me, I tucked the volume under my arm and continued up the hill, feeling somehow that I was being watched. Was Gabe keeping tabs on me or being overly dramatic? Was Gates lurking around? It wasn't until I was safely in my office that I looked closely at the book he had given me. As I picked up the copy of *Weightlifting for the Pros*—a book I didn't own but couldn't wait to read—a small slip of paper dropped onto the floor.

"Del need to sea you. Tonite. 10 p.m. Irrish Band Bridge."

15

Before I moved to Oregon, I thought that covered bridges were characteristic only of New England. It was a pleasant surprise to discover that Oregon had a lot of these graceful wooden structures too. The earliest one had been built in 1919 and by the 1920s, the state boasted over four hundred. But their construction was not for romantic reasons. Because Oregon has always had so much rain, the bridges served a practical function: their roofs kept wooden decks and trusses from rotting so quickly.

In the decades since, weather and insects had destroyed many of the bridges, which were also abandoned because they could not handle the heavy traffic of modern times. By the time I saw my first covered bridge, most were falling down.

Then, suddenly, a lot of them were being demolished to make way for more modern structures. You couldn't pick up a paper in the late 1970s and early 1980s and not read about such destruction, always couched in phrases using the word "progress."

At the same time, however, word came of parallel activity: private efforts to save covered bridges either by constructing bypasses and having the bridge become a bike path, or by moving the structure to an entirely different location.

The latter is what happened when the covered bridge at Irish Bend in a rural area of western Oregon was scheduled to be torn down to accommodate a highway expansion. The bridge was saved, however, when private funds were used to move it to an undeveloped site on campus to the west of the cow and sheep barns.

In its new location, the bridge covered part of a bike/jogging path. Visitors were free to walk through it and observe its construction of huge fir planks and steel cables. They could enjoy its simple beauty. If they closed their eyes, they might almost hear the clatter of horses' hooves and carriage wheels or the sputtering of a Model T engine.

It was to this pleasant spot that I now made my way, wondering if the bridge would seem as romantic in total darkness.

I left my office at about nine fifteen to allow plenty of time to keep my appointment with Del. I decided to walk because private cars weren't permitted in this part of campus so I felt my own would attract too much attention. I didn't question his need to see me. Something must have changed for him to risk discovery and, possibly, arrest by police in Corvallis.

I have never been afraid to walk on campus after dark, reports of occasional muggings and rapes notwithstanding. I must admit, however, that I seldom walked around at night. This late, only a fool would fail to notice that the many shrubs and bushes around buildings make excellent hiding places for anyone waiting to prey on the solitary stroller or jogger.

I headed out of my building via the north entrance then turned left and walked across the plaza area to Campus Way. Turning left again, I continued along past the buildings housing home economics, the extension service and ag engineering.

Ahead of me at this point loomed the new Agricultural and Life Science Building on the left with its sky bridge to Cordley Hall on the right. As an under-funded program that didn't bring in many research funds, journalism was doomed to old and rather shabby quarters. I envied the newness of the classrooms I was passing with built-in audiovisual equipment and good acoustics in lecture halls.

Next I passed the horticulture greenhouses and walked on by the building housing animal science, rangeland resource, and the university theatre. Only here would these three widely varying endeavors be keeping company under the same roof. The odd juxtaposition had happened for budgetary reasons after the old playhouse in the center of campus had been condemned.

I paused on NW 30th to let a car roar by. In spite of the cold night, its top was down and the men and women jammed into it were feeling no pain. They were yelling various obscenities and singing the Fight Song. After the car sped by me, someone threw a bottle out of the vehicle. It hit a tree in the median and broke into hundreds of pieces.

"Way to go!" one of them yelled.

"Idiots," I muttered to myself as I crossed the street.

In a half block, I reached the motor pool, which was bathed in floodlight. Then I heard a clanking sound to my left, which startled me.

"Lost, mister?" I jumped as a strong beam of a flashlight pierced the darkness surrounding me. I stopped, glad that I had changed into jogging clothes to prepare for just such an encounter. I never jogged but I had clothing on that said I did. All I lacked was sweat on my brow.

The light moved toward me, the figure of a campus security guard behind it.

"Good evening, officer. No, I'm from campus. I teach here. I like to jog on campus after the crowds are gone. It helps clear my head."

The young officer shined his light up and down my body, then turned it off.

"Greg Miller. How ya doin'?"

"Good, Officer Miller, maybe a bit cold."

We shook hands and I changed the subject.

"Some trouble at the motor pool?"

"No, not really. We recently caught that guy who'd been stealing PCs from here and a lot of other departments. That sucker is locked up. I just keep my eye on this place because of all the cars. I come by here every half hour or so."

"Oh. Yeah. That seems like a good idea."

At this point, we had exhausted our areas of mutual interest, but I didn't want to be too abrupt, lest he suspect that I wasn't a real jogger.

"How 'bout those Beavers?"

It was time for my old sports fan ploy. Officer Miller rose quickly to the bait and chatted for a minute or two about how he thought the university team would do in the PAC-10 basketball season then about half over.

He made the first move to leave, glancing at his watch as he held his wrist up toward the nearest floodlight.

"Wow. Nine forty. I'm late. It's been nice talking to you, sir. Have a nice night—and a good jog."

"Same here. Goodnight, Officer Miller."

I started running in place the same way I had seen runners do on television. Then, in a burst of authenticity I jogged off looking, I hoped, athletic. I stopped running as soon as I cleared the lighted area. He hadn't asked my name, which was good. If nothing startling came of this night, I hoped he would soon forget me entirely or at least precisely where and when he had seen me.

Soon I crossed NW 35th Street and entered a part of campus that keeps the university tied to its origins as a land grant university. On my right was the sheep barn, its inhabitants bleating loudly at this late hour.

The beef barn next to it was quiet, although I heard an occasional moo as I hurried by. There was no mistaking the smell of manure, however. Miraculously, that scent seldom found its way to main campus. The prevailing breezes kept it out here. Once in a while, however, especially on damp nights, we all remember why our rivals call us a cow college.

The moon was high in the sky as I left the area of buildings. I looked up and marveled at the clarity of the starry night. I hunched up my shoulders and rubbed my upper arms because of the cold.

After another five minutes on the path, I could see the bridge ahead of me, its distinct shape glistening in the surprisingly bright light of the moon. I stopped to enjoy the view.

In a minute or two, my reverie was interrupted by the sound of a thud, then footsteps running away from the bridge. It sounded like something had hit the timbers. I ran toward the structure, then thought I heard an engine starting up in the distance. First one, then another—maybe motorcycles. I listened carefully but the vehicles seemed to be going in the opposite direction, probably continuing along Campus Way to NW 53rd Street, the outer western boundary of campus.

I reached the bridge and started across it, my footsteps echoing on its wooden floor planks. I stopped in the middle to listen, but detected nothing except the faint mooing and bleating I had already heard. I looked up through the open sides of the bridge and saw the beautiful night.

"Del. Del Johnson."

I used a stage whisper although I was sure no one was around.

"Are you here? It's Tom Martindale. I'm alone. It's safe to come out."

Nothing.

I reached for a small flashlight I had been keeping in the pocket of my sweatshirt and shined it around the bridge. I walked to the end, then, on a hunch, walked down the sides of the culvert. Maybe Del was hiding down there to make sure I was really alone.

"Del."

I dared to raise my voice to somewhere below a shout. I kept moving down and then shined my light to the point where the support beams of the bridge intersected with the ground.

"Oh shit."

Duke Ramsay's body was twisting slowly in the slight breeze. The academic adviser who kept athletes eligible over the years was certainly dead, his limp form hanging by a heavy chain that was cutting savagely into his neck.

16

knew enough not to touch Ramsay's body. I felt weak in the knees as I looked at him, but knew I had to get help. My first thought after I stumbled up the embankment was to get back to the motor pool and officer what's-his-name. I couldn't recall it at the moment, but it would come to me. Even if I couldn't find him, there was a pay phone at the edge of the parking lot.

I hurried across the bridge and down the path to the sheep and cow barn area. The lights were out in the sheep enclosure, or else I would have stopped to look for a telephone. All was quiet except for an occasional noise inside those buildings.

It took me seven minutes to reach the motor pool. I didn't see the security guard anywhere so I stepped into the phone booth and dialed 9-1-1.

"9-1-1 emergency."

"I just found a body under the Irish Bend Bridge."

Your name, sir?"

"Tom Martindale."

"How do you know this person is dead?"

"He is hanging."

"It is a male decedent, then?"

"Yes. A man. As I was saying, he is hanging by a chain from one of the support beams under the bridge. He wasn't moving."

"All right, sir. We will send an officer to you. Where are you?"

"The pay phone next to the motor pool on Campus Way."

"All right, sir. Stay where you are."

"I'll wait for him here."

At that moment, the security guard's car turned into the parking lot. I motioned for him to come over to me.

"Boy, officer, am I glad to see you!"

I quickly glanced at the name plate on his uniform.

"Officer Miller. Do you remember me from earlier?"

"Yes, sir, I do. You're the jogger I spoke to at about nine thirty or so."

"That's right. That's me. My name is Tom Martindale."

"What's the matter? You look upset."

"I found a body out on the jogging path. I just called 9-1-1 to report it. I came back here looking for you."

"A body? Whereabouts?"

"Under the Irish Bend Bridge."

"Show me. Get in the car and guide me there."

"The 9-1-1 dispatcher told me to wait for an officer."

"I am an officer, sir. Let's get moving. I'll call in and tell them there's been a change of plans."

I followed him somewhat reluctantly because I knew that there were two levels of security on campus. The Oregon State Police had overall jurisdiction and handled the heavy duty stuff. The campus security force—Officer Miller included—looked after traffic control and building security, like checking to see if doors and gates were locked.

We got in his car and he sped down the street. He seemed to be enjoying himself immensely. Looking over crime scenes certainly beat trying doors and padlocks I suppose.

"Do you know the victim?"

If I lied, I might be putting myself in hot water later, but I didn't really want to be dragged into this investigation either. I equivocated like crazy.

"It was really dark under there. I may have seen him before. I just couldn't be sure."

"I suppose he's in pretty bad shape."

Could Miller be getting a real thrill out of this? Was this the first body he had to deal with?

"I didn't look too closely."

We were driving onto the path, past the cow and sheep barns and the sign that said "Emergency Vehicles Only." I glanced over at Miller's face. He was smiling. This had to be his first big case.

"Follow the path up over that rise and you'll see the bridge."

On cue, the graceful structure loomed ahead, its wide fir planks illuminated by the headlights. Miller pulled up to the bridge and turned off the ignition.

"Car twenty-one. Please respond."

Miller paid no attention to the staccato blasts from the radio. Maybe this wasn't car twenty-one.

"Car twenty-one. Officer Miller. Please respond."

Miller looked at me and smiled, rather gleefully, I thought.

"Should you take that call and tell them were we are?"

"I need to check things out first. Come on. Show me where the body is."

We both got out of the car. As we walked to the other end of the bridge, I heard the radio give one more futile blast.

"God damn it, Greg. Where the hell are you?"

A man's voice had replaced that of the female dispatcher. Miller paid no attention, pushing ahead of me, eager to see that body.

I stopped at the top of the embankment and pointed.

"Down there."

"Show me exactly."

I nodded and stepped carefully down the incline, Miller close behind me. I turned and looked up under the bridge. From where I stopped, only Ramsay's shoe was visible to the rays of my flashlight.

"There. It's up there."

Miller pushed ahead of me, practically knocking me down in his eagerness to get to the body.

"Here, take my light, then shine both yours and mine on the body."

I did what I was told, as Miller stepped up on one of the lower supports in order to reach up and touch the body.

"Shouldn't you wait for someone who knows . . . for someone to help you?"

"Look, Professor Martindale is it?"

I nodded.

"I'm a fully trained security officer. I'm perfectly able to analyze the crime scene before I call it in."

"All right. I guess you know best."

"Damn right, I do. Now, step in closer with those lights."

I did as I was told and shined the flashlights directly onto Ramsay's body. Miller was apparently trying to get a pulse although even a civilian like me could see that Duke's heart had long since ceased to beat. As the officer groped for the vein in Ramsay's neck, he lost his footing and grabbed onto the chain for support. For a moment or two, the two figures hung there, Miller pawing the air, Duke looking grotesque.

"Miller. What in the hell do you think you're doing?"

The voice behind us was familiar. Before I could turn around, Duke Ramsay's body and the hapless Miller came crashing down, coming to rest in front of me and the polished boots of Lieutenant Angela Pride.

"I find you in the damnedest places," Angela said to me.

She looked down at Miller and shook her head. She raised an arm to summon others in her entourage.

"Pat, can you help bring some order to this mess?"

Miller was trying to stand but he was all tangled up in Ramsay's arms and legs, which seemed to have wrapped themselves around him in the fall. He looked miserable. Pride motioned for me to follow her up the embankment. We walked to her car, which was parked on the path at the other end of the bridge.

"Get in and let's talk, Tom."

"What's this all about, Tom?" she asked as we closed the car doors. "What are you involved with this time?"

"I swear, I'm as pure as the proverbial driven snow. I was jogging out here to clear my head after a tough week and . . ."

"Yeah. Nice clothes. They look new. Haven't had the time to do any marathons yet, I guess. Somehow, you never struck me as someone who would like to get all out of breath and sweaty."

"At least not from jogging."

A little humor never hurt anything, but Angela wasn't smiling. It was a bad joke, given our past history.

"So you were at least walking fast, if not jogging?"

I nodded.

"So why out here and so late at night?"

"It's too busy earlier—all those cows and sheep to wade through. I didn't get to my jog until late. I had class and a committee meeting and papers to grade."

"Okay, I got it. You're busy! But it's Friday night, Tom."

"Oh, you know how it is, Angela. No rest for the wicked and all that stuff."

I suddenly felt chilled; the effects of seeing Ramsay's battered body were probably settling in.

"Can you turn the heater up a bit?"

"Sure, Tom." She looked at me. "You all right? Don't go into shock on me."

She reached behind me and placed a thermos bottle on the console between us and unscrewed the top, then poured some steaming liquid into the top and handed it to me.

"Here. It's strong coffee. I ground the beans myself. Drink it slowly. It'll warm you up."

"Thanks."

We sat in silence for a few minutes while I sipped my coffee. We could see the others going about their tasks in the headlights of several vehicles pulled up to the top of the embankment. Miller came up in a few minutes, brushing himself off. He said something to another state policeman who pointed toward Pride's car. Miller walked toward us.

"This sorry bastard probably wants my forgiveness," Pride said under her breath.

She rolled down the window slightly. Miller leaned down.

"Lieutenant Pride. I don't know what to say. I blew it."

"Yes, Miller, you did. You compromised the crime scene, you didn't follow procedure, you big footed into something you don't know anything about."

"I know, I know. I just . . ."

"You just what, Miller? Kissed your law enforcement career goodbye? You got that right!" Pride's voice was colder than I had ever heard it.

"Now get out of here and get cleaned up. You're suspended from duty until further notice."

With that, Pride rolled the window up and turned her back on Miller, who looked like a puppy abandoned in the middle of a freeway.

I sipped the coffee. Pride was right: it was helping me focus.

"Don't you think you were a bit hard on him, Angela?"

Pride didn't say anything but looked straight ahead.

"Is he really finished?"

"He's a nice kid, if a bit over-eager. But I need to teach him a lesson over this case. But he probably isn't finished. I'll just have to keep him on a short leash for a while."

"I'm glad. He is kind of a doofus but I don't get the impression that he means any harm."

"All right, Tom. Let's quit this bullshitting. Are you going to tell me what you were doing out here or do I have to take drastic measures with you too?"

I nodded, quickly running the situation through my numbed brain. If I told her about Del Johnson and the note I got to meet him here, that would turn suspicion toward him and implicate me in aiding a fugitive. If, on the other hand, I came up with a different scenario, I could buy some time by diverting attention elsewhere.

"Well, Tom."

"I was to meet Duke Ramsay out here, but he was dead when I got here."

"Now, we're getting somewhere. I'm all ears."

"I had lunch with him several days ago. I've known him for years so I called him to fish for details on the athletic department and how it keeps its athletes eligible. Duke is . . . was . . . the head adviser down there so I knew he'd know a lot. I'm interested in this because I think black athletes are not being well-served. Grade records may have been falsified, I'm not sure. I think the whole situation down there somehow got Emily Morgan killed."

"Now hold on a minute, Tom. That's a pretty big leap—from helping jocks pass courses to killing a coed."

"I know. I haven't put it all together yet. It seems like a stretch but I think I'm right. And something else, Angela. Del Johnson did not kill Emily. They loved one another."

"They loved one another and she got pregnant and he did not want a baby, etc., etc. I am sure you can fill in the missing parts of that scenario."

"You're wrong, Angela. I know it looks bad but I know him. You're looking for the wrong guy while the real killer or killers are getting away."

She shook her head. "This isn't getting us anywhere. Let's get back to Duke, your old pal who's dead down there under the bridge. What did he tell you at lunch?"

I filled her in on what Ramsay had said and also told her about our encounter with the two athletes in the parking lot.

"Did you get their names?"

"One was Bobby Hardy. The other kid . . ."

"Hardy. Bobby is the first name, you say?"

I nodded.

"Why does that ring a bell?"

"He was the kid you found huddled in the steam tunnel last night."

"And how did you make that connect . . . Don't tell me, Tom. You were in there with him."

I got red in the face and took another sip of coffee before answering. I nodded hesitantly.

"Good God, Tom! Where won't I find traces of you in this case? Do you realize that you're blundering into things that don't concern you—things that could get you killed?"

"I know. I'm sorry but . . ."

"But, nothing. If you don't stay out of this, I'm going to your chairman, then the dean, and even the president if I have to!"

"Okay, I hear you. Let me finish my story. I was in there because he chased me in there!"

"And why, pray tell, did he do that?"

"He caught me spying on him in the pool."

"Is this going to get kinky, Tom? Where are you heading with this?"

"Not where you think. What happened was I was leaving my office and saw Hardy and a woman going into the men's gym so I followed them."

"So it's against the rules to take your lady friend for a midnight . . ."

"It was more like ten thirty or so."

"Figure of speech, wise ass. A night swim is no crime."

"Yeah, but it does raise questions when your swimming partner is the wife of your coach."

Angela spit out some coffee she was just then drinking. It dribbled down her immaculate uniform. She immediately began to dab at the spots with a napkin.

"Now that is too much of a leap even for you! I hate to say it, Tom, but you may be losing it."

"Let me continue, Angela."

She waved a hand at me to go on, a look of disgust still on her face.

"Something Duke told me at lunch got me to thinking that maybe Gloria Martino plays more than just footsy with some of the players. So when I saw them together, I decided to follow them into the building."

"And, what happened?"

"Skinny dipping was the least of it."

"In a public pool with the chance for someone to find them? I don't believe it. You're outdoing yourself this time, Tom."

"I saw what I saw, Angela."

I pointed to my eyes for emphasis.

"They were about to do a little screwing in the water. They heard me, I ran, he followed, and you know the rest."

"What happened to the missus?"

"After leaving the tunnel, I waited for the police to arrive. Well, before that happened, she left the building walking pretty fast. She couldn't have cared less about her young boyfriend."

Pride shook her head. The lack of an outburst made me think that she was beginning to believe me. I decided it was best to keep quiet about talking to Gloria Martino myself.

"Why would any of this connect to the Morgan girl?"

"I don't know, but I think there is some kind of link."

"I'm going to take your word that you've told me everything you know about this."

I nodded, crossing the fingers of my right hand, resting in the seat where she couldn't see it. That gesture always absolved shaders of the truth like me from future divine retribution—didn't it?

"And you will leave the detective work to me from now on?"

I hesitated and she laughed.

"Or you will at least tell me everything you find out?"

I smiled and nodded again.

"That goes without saying, Angela. We want the same thing."

She looked at her watch.

"God, it's nearly one. Do you want me to get someone to drive you to your car?"

"No. I need to unwind. I'd like to walk back. The walk will make me sleep well. I don't have to get up early tomorrow. It's Saturday, thank God. Can I call you next week to see how things are going with the investigation about Duke?"

"Sure. And I need a full statement soon! You said you had that ad shoot or something coming up Monday?"

"Yeah. Monday and Tuesday. After that, I'll be free."

We shook hands and both got out of the car. Angela headed toward the bridge and the group of officers working there. An ambulance was just backing up to the edge of the embankment.

I headed in the other direction. It felt good to be in the cold air and I took deep breaths every so often to cleanse my lungs. I passed the sheep and cow barns without incident. I crossed the street and made my way past the motor pool. The frost on the tops of cars and vans inside the fence glistened in the light.

I had crossed NW 30th and was in front of the greenhouses when I caught a glimpse of someone standing in the moonlight to my left.

17

Del was dressed completely in black, from his jogging pants to his sweatshirt, the hood of which he had pulled down so it partially covered his face. We both quickly headed farther back into the safety of the greenhouse complex. Unfortunately, it was not completely dark inside the glass walled buildings. Horticulture experiments went on around the clock so there were lights on here and there

"There's a live-in attendant over in that building," Del whispered and pointed to the next building."

"Over there." I pointed to an area of darkness toward Cordley Hall where we could converse for a minute or two without being observed.

"Whew. All this sneaking around gets the old adrenaline pumping."

Del looked tired and a bit frightened.

"I'm glad to see you're all right. Let's go to my office right now. If we sit in the dark, no one will see us or, at this hour, bother us."

He nodded, looking a bit dubious.

"Trust me. No one will be there. Let's do it now."

We moved quickly along and crossed the brick plaza that led to the side of my building. I touched his arm and pointed to some tall bushes at the end of the building. He nodded and disappeared behind them. As casually as I could I walked into the glare of the street light, got out my key, and opened the door. In an instant, Del Johnson sprinted by me into the building.

The lights were off in most parts of this lower hall. Only the fire exit signs glowed here and there as they indicated exits in the long building. He walked up the stairs and turned to go down the second floor hall to the safety of my office.

I didn't turn on any lights in either the conference room or the office beyond it. I locked both doors and guided him to a chair opposite my desk. I raised the blind so we could get a small amount of light from outside.

"You can relax here, Del. You're safe. Take off your sweatshirt if you want. It's boiling hot in here."

I bent down to turn the knob on the steam heat radiator in front of the window. The hissing subsided but the radiator started popping loudly as it cooled down. I was finally feeling warm.

"Let's talk. What happened out there at that bridge?"

"Aren't you going to ask me if I killed Mr. Ramsay?" I didn't answer.

"I parked my car way out along 53rd and walked in to the bridge about nine. No one was around so I hid out in one of the sheds. It had hay and stuff in it. I guess to feed the animals. I figured you'd be walking out there since you can't drive cars on that path. I thought I'd catch you as you went by."

"When you crossed the bridge, did you see or hear anything?"

"Yeah. That's why I ran. About fifteen minutes after I got there, Mr. Ramsay came walking the path. He looked real scared. I mean he kept looking all around, even up in the sky, like he thought some giant hand might pluck him up off the ground."

"He was a jumpy guy. Go on."

"He went by and I stayed hidden, wondering whether I should wait for you or split. I mean I didn't want him to see me. He was a nice guy—helpful to the athletes and all that—but I didn't want to risk him turning me in. I didn't trust him with my life, that's for damn sure!"

"So what happened next?"

"In less than five minutes, I heard him cry out something like, 'Who are you? What do you want? Get away from me.' Then I heard a thud."

"What kind of thud?"

"Like wood against bone. I was just a kid in the L.A. riots after the Rodney King verdict. I heard that same sound when the cops came through South Central where I lived and used their batons to hit people over the head. I'll always remember that sound."

"Did you investigate—I mean did you walk over toward the sound?"

"No way, man. Do you think I'm crazy? I got out of there fast. I figured whatever happened was nothing I needed to be anywhere near."

"But you hung around to see if you could find me?"

"Yeah, in the trees. I positioned myself where I could observe the bridge easily without being seen," Del said.

"When I got near the bridge, I heard what sounded like motorcycles— maybe two of them—starting up. They drove away from me and I never saw anything. I looked around on the bridge, then under it and that's where I found Duke Ramsay's body.

"I figured it was him. I couldn't see much. But I saw the police come. First you and the one guy, then later the whole crew. Why did that first guy jump up on the body that way?" Del asked.

"You saw that?"

"Yeah. You were holding two flashlights on him. It lit things up pretty well."

"Oh, he was overeager, trying to be a state cop instead of a security guard. He really messed up the crime scene in the process. Do you know anyone who drives a motorcycle?"

He thought for a few minutes, then answered hesitantly.

"Kurt Blake."

"Why does that name sound familiar?"

"I mentioned it to you the other day when we were talking about where Emily and I were the night she was killed."

Oh yeah. He was with Bobby Hardy and Mrs. Martino at the restaurant, wasn't he? You said he's her nephew?"

Del nodded. "He's not a member of the team but he hangs out with us."

"He has a motorcycle?"

"Yeah, it's his pride and joy."

"How about someone else? It sounded like two machines to me."

"No one I know about. Most of the guys drive sports cars. Bobby Hardy used to work in a motorcycle shop in Portland when he was in high school but I've never seen him riding one. He told me about it a long time ago."

"So maybe those two guys killed Duke Ramsay."

"Maybe, but why would they do it? Mr. Ramsay was nice to all the players."

He thought for a minute.

"Unless maybe he resented all the attention Mr. Ramsay paid to black players. There was an incident about six months ago, in some class Hardy and Gabe Washington were in. The teacher accused both of them of cheating on the exam. Gabe denied it and blamed Bobby for it. Mr. Ramsay took Gabe's part. Hardy was really pissed for a while, then he seemed to get over it."

"So he might have sought revenge?"

"I don't know if I'd go that far. I mean he's not a racist—at least never to me. I suppose it's possible he held a grudge, though."

"Have you seen Gloria Martino?"

"Not since the night Emily was murdered. Why do you ask? You still think I am sleeping with her, don't you?"

"No, not really. I thought maybe she had tried to get in touch with you?"

"Nobody knows where I am but you and Gabe. You have to believe me on that. Nobody!"

"I believe you. Sorry to have upset you. I'm just trying to figure out what happened."

Del looked awful and I hated to lay anything else on him now, but I had to.

"Del, there's something else I have to ask you. How long have you known that Emily was carrying your baby?"

Del jumped to his feet, a look of pure astonishment on his face.

"Baby! What baby? I don't know anything about any baby! Emily was pregnant? Oh, my God. Poor Em."

And then he started to cry, his big shoulders heaving up and down with each sob.

"I'm sorry to drop this on you. I thought she had told you."

"She told you, and not me?" He looked up in disbelief and wiped his eyes with his hand.

"No, no. The autopsy showed she was about two months along."

"That would be about right—I mean before we broke up. God, why didn't she tell me?"

"The last night—she didn't say anything?"

"She didn't say a word. That would have changed everything. I would have married her right away, even with all the problems we'd have down the road."

Del took out a handkerchief and blew his nose.

"You've got to realize that her being pregnant makes you a more likely suspect."

He nodded and looked down at the floor.

"What are you going to do, Del? Would you consider turning yourself into the police? I know Lieutenant Pride here on campus. She's a fair person. I'll see that you are treated fairly."

"You've got to be kidding. They'll fry me for sure because of this."

"How long can you stay in that house in Salem?"

"Not much longer. The walls are closing in."

"Any place else you can go?"

"Gabe's got relatives in Portland—in the Albina area. It's predominantly African-American. I'll be safe there for a while. Gabe will know where I am."

"I've been trying to find out who killed Emily. I intend to clear your name."

He looked at me with what looked, in the dim light from the window, like tears in his eyes. "Thanks, Professor Martindale. Thanks a lot."

We shook hands solemnly.

Just then, a vehicle came to an abrupt stop outside. I peered out the window.

"It's the police! You've got to get out of here! Come on. I've got an idea."

I turned on the light and grabbed my trash can. He followed me through the next set of fire doors. Just inside those door was the opening to the ancient trash chute that ran down to a dumpster located in a utility room on the first floor.

"Climb in here. It'll be close but I think you'll fit. Hold on until you hear me talking to them, then let yourself slide down. You'll land in a dumpster and then you can walk quietly out the back and into the night. Once you're out of the building, you'll know how to disappear."

"Thanks."

He climbed in feet first and held on as we waited for the police.

I winked at him and started making exaggerated thumps on my trash can to cover any noise he made in his descent. Del slipped from view and I closed the door to the chute. The two officers had turned on the hall lights and were walking toward me, their hands on their radios, I suppose to summon reinforcements if necessary. They carried no guns. I opened the fire doors and walked as nonchalantly as I could toward them.

"Good evening, officers. What can I do for you?"

"Who are you and what are you doing here?" one barked. "We got a call about an intruder."

"I'm Tom Martindale. I teach journalism and this is my office." I gestured toward the open door and the lighted room beyond. I pulled out and showed them my after-hours building permit.

"I was just dumping the trash before going home." I yawned in an exaggerated way. "It's really getting late. I'm calling it a day. Is there a problem?"

"Sorry to have bothered you," murmured the one who hadn't yet spoken.

18

SATURDAY

I slept later than usual the next morning. I even took my phone off the hook so I wouldn't be disturbed. It had been a rough week.

I had bought my condominium when I first moved to town. It was just the right size for me: living room with adjacent dining area, kitchen, bathroom, and two bedrooms, one of which I used as an office. I had built floor-to-ceiling bookshelves there and enjoyed working at an old oak table I had placed in front of a window. From here I had a good view of the forested slopes of the Coast Range on the edge of town.

I planned to spend the next two days at home working on the advertising script and getting my lecture notes ready. I wouldn't have much time to prepare for class in the hectic week ahead.

As I ate breakfast, I thought about Del. I assumed he got away. With all the attention focused on me, it had probably been fairly easy.

I washed the dishes and ran the vacuum. I started a load of washing, then settled down for a second cup of coffee at the kitchen table. I reached over and placed the receiver back on the base of the phone, as I had done earlier for the extension in the bedroom. It immediately rang.

"Tom? Angela Pride here. Boy you've really been gabbing a long time to somebody this morning."

"Morning, Angela. I hate to admit it, but I took the damn thing off the hook so I could get some sleep this morning."

"It's nearly eleven now, so I assume you've gotten all the beauty sleep you need."

"Yeah. I feel pretty good, especially for someone who's been tracking dead people all night."

"That's why I called. I wanted to let you know how your friend Duke Ramsay was killed."

"Yeah, I'm interested to hear."

"His neck was broken before whoever killed him strung him up. Then his killer hit him on the head with a blunt object to finish the job."

"Angela, did you ever wonder why people associated with the football team were suddenly turning up dead?"

"That's kind of farfetched, Tom. Our team doesn't always win, but I don't think people are upset enough to kill over it," she chuckled.

"Yeah, I guess not."

I joined in the laughter at the ridiculousness of the idea.

"Pretty stupid thought, I guess."

"I've got to run. I'm due in Salem at a commander's meeting."

"On Saturday? Angela, you're working too hard."

"Knowing you, Tom, I'll bet you brought a full briefcase home, too."

"Guilty. Oh, one more thing. Can you assign an officer to be around when we're shooting next week? I'm not expecting any trouble, but I'd feel better if someone at least looked in now and then."

"Done. I'll take care of it. Fax me the locations for your shoots."

After I hung up, I poured another cup of coffee and sat at the big table I use for a desk in my study. When I get involved in things that seem to be spinning out of control, I try to sit quietly like this so I can think. These days, that simple activity is very under-used. More people should try it; it does wonders in clearing the head.

The Emily Morgan and Duke Ramsay murders intersected at the athletic department, or more specifically with the football program. Who had these two people crossed that cost them their lives? Murder is a fairly drastic step for anyone to even contemplate, let alone carry out. In the buttoned down world of a university, it was unthinkable. Yet, it had happened—twice.

I turned on my computer and waited for it to boot up and go through its various gyrations to get me on line. Maybe a Nexus search would get me some useful information. I typed in the first name I was interested in: Ricardo Martino.

The football coach had been at several schools before coming to campus two years ago. I waited and soon had thirty-six "Ricardo Martino's" blinking back at me from the screen.

I punched in "Oregon University" and "football" and immediately got what I wanted. There were 13 entries in this configuration and I brought them up in chronological order.

The first entry dealt with the coach's own college career. The next four detailed his two years on a professional team, the San Diego Chargers. These stories were mostly about specific games and they chronicled the activities of a good, but not great player, according to the *San Diego Tribune*'s sports columnist. I was ready to shift ahead to the start of Martino's coaching career when a cross-reference caught my eye.

"See also Martino, Gloria."

Odd that his wife would be listed in this manner in his bio stuff. Perhaps it was a wedding announcement. I brought it up and soon saw that it was far from a notice of the Martino's marriage.

PLAYER FINDS INTRUDER
IN HIS LA JOLLA HOME

San Diego Chargers Fullback Ricardo "Ricky" Martino got more than he bargained for when he returned home last night from an extended road trip. An intruder was holding his wife against her will in their La Jolla home.

Martino, 28, quickly subdued the man, Chad Elkins, 21, a senior at San Diego Sate University, and called police. No one was injured in the incident.

Gloria Martino, 27, told police that she had awakened to find Elkins going through drawers in the bedroom. The Martino's infant daughter, Lucinda, slept through the entire incident.

Elkins, who has a record of arrests for possession of marijuana, will be arraigned tomorrow in San Diego District Court.

"Yeah, right. I bet he was going through your drawers all right, Mrs. M," I muttered to myself.

I brought up more stories dealing with Gloria Martino. In over half of them, however, she was referred to by her maiden name, Gloria Sinclair. Two years after the Elkins incident, she had been involved in a minor traffic accident while leaving a motel parking lot in Mobile, Alabama; Martino had by this time become an assistant coach at the University of Alabama. This time, another "intruder" was seen by witnesses running from her car after the accident. She said she had given a ride to a hitchhiker who was taking a nap in the back seat.

"I don't believe this stuff! She ought to go into fiction writing."

I was muttering again as I trolled through the past lives of both Martinos. No more incidents made the papers until last year, when Oregon State Police had stopped her for speeding. This time, a member of the football team had been in the car with her—Bobby Hardy, 19. Another young man, Kurt Blake, 29, described as her nephew, had also been in the car. Both men had failed breathalizer tests. Mrs. Martino had not been drinking, however, so was cited only for driving at an excessive speed.

I printed out all of these stories. What was I seeing here? A woman who apparently preferred the company of young studs to that of her husband? That fit the pattern I had heard about from Duke and Del and what I had observed in the swimming pool.

She had apparently carried on like this throughout their marriage. Why her husband ignored it was anyone's guess, but how did the search committee miss it? Amateur athletics exists in no small part because of the willingness of donors to keep giving money. Here, many of those donors were alumni. Most are talented, intelligent, prosperous, even sophisticated people. Few would look favorably on a coach whose wife made the news too often.

I returned to a search of Coach Martino's file. Other clippings covered his career as an assistant at Alabama and time as head coach at the University of Montana. Everything seemed routine until I brought up a story from his last year there.

COACH WOUNDS TRANSIENT
IN MOUNTAIN CABIN FRACAS

University of Montana football coach Ricardo "Ricky" Martino shot and wounded a transient he found living in his mountain cabin near St. Ignatius early yesterday.

Martino, 39, head coach of the Grizzlies since last year, said he had come out to the cabin to check reports from neighbors of a break-in. He arrived at about 3 a.m. and found the intruder asleep in the living room. The two argued and Martino shot the intruder in the arm when he came at him with a fireplace poker.

The transient, Kurt Blake, 26, of San Diego, California was treated and released from Mercy Hospital. Martino did not press charges.

Well, well. Funny that Gloria Martino's "nephew" would get shot for staying at his aunt's cabin. "Nephew" my ass. He's involved in some kind of off-again, on-again relationship with Gloria. But why would Martino put up with this? And why was he hired with such a public record of past incidents? Did Gloria have something on Martino that kept him covering up for her?

I scrolled on.

OSU FOOTBALL COACH BUYS
INTEREST IN COASTAL INN

Oregon University's new assistant football coach has purchased a minority interest in the Cape Foulweather Inn, a bed and breakfast on the Oregon Coast. Ricardo "Ricky" Martino, 41, said that he wanted to diversify his sources of income to pave the way for his eventual retirement.

"I love Oregon and I love the Oregon Coast," he said. "My wife is from Albany and we have always wanted to return to the state to live."

Martino came to campus last year and has been trying to improve on the team's 3-35 record over the past three seasons.

Partners in the purchase of the fifty-year-old inn are Gregory Hapgood, a Portland attorney, Elliot White, a Portland stockbroker, and Kurt Blake, a relative of Mrs. Martino, the former Gloria Sinclair.

The new owners assumed control last week and immediately begin a $500,000 renovation of the building which overlooks the Pacific Ocean from the highest point on the Central Oregon Coast.

Blake again. Why did he keep reappearing in the Martino's lives? And why would you take on as partner a man you had shot only two years before? It sure beat the hell out of me. Also, Elliot White was one of the big contributors Ramsay had mentioned.

I turned off the computer and finished my, by now, ice cold coffee. I looked in my Staff Directory for a number and dialed.

"Skip? Tom Martindale. How are you?"

"Yes, Tom. Why are you calling me at home?"

Skip Olson was a lot less friendly than he had been at the committee meeting.

"What's this about? I've got my in-laws here."

Olson's voice had dropped a tone or two so that I could barely hear him.

"I won't keep you long, Skip. I need to ask you a question about the assistant head coach. If I'm not mistaken, you were a member of the search committee that hired him."

"Why ask me? I don't know Gloria Martino very well at all."

"No, Skip. You didn't hear my question. I said Coach Martino, not his wife. The assistant coach, Ricky Martino."

"What does this have to do with our image committee or whatever bullshit name it has?"

"Skip, Skip. Come in, please. Not our committee, the search committee you were on for the coach. I think you were a member."

There was a long silence on the other end.

"Oh yeah, sure," he answered vaguely. "I was thrilled to serve on it. How our teams do is very important to our alums. When they are happy with the football team, they tend to give more to the university. Plus, I'm a real sports fanatic."

Olson was now back to his usual bonhomie.

"I think we made the right choice, don't you? Ricky Martino is a fine man and a great coach. He'll make a great replacement for Coach Brewster when he decides to retire."

"And what about Gloria Martino? Is she a fine woman?"

"How would I know that, Tom?" laughed Olson.

"You mentioned her name first, that's why. I thought you were talking about her. My wife has met . . ."

"Never mind, Skip. I get the picture."

"Now what was it you called me for?"

"Just curious about the search process. I am trying to teach my students new ways to find information by using their computers. You guys used Nexus to get stuff on Martino's background, didn't you?"

"We checked some of his references, but after we met Ricky, Gloria, and their two lovely children, we had all we needed. We made a great choice. Don't you agree, Tom?

"Great. Yeah. Well, I shouldn't keep you from your in-laws."

19

The western third of Oregon—its beautiful coastline and towns located along the Pacific Ocean—is separated from the more populated Willamette Valley by a relatively low string of mountains called, appropriately enough, the Coast Range. The route over the mountains was a familiar one because it was the quickest way to get to the coast, an area I try to visit as often as I can.

I spent my sabbatical in a house in Newport about ten years ago and have been saving ever since for a place of my own along the rugged shoreline. For me, there is no more inspirational place in the world to write than a room with an ocean view.

The road from Corvallis to Newport, Oregon Highway 20, is a sometimes twisting, turning thoroughfare that can be dangerous if you aren't careful. There are few places to pass another car safely, so I never do.

After talking to Skip Olson, and reading the Nexus printout, I decided on a whim to drive to Martino's inn and have a look around. Because no one really knew who I was, I hoped I could wander in and not arouse suspicion.

The people of the coast are always casual, but I hated feeling like a tourist so I had dressed a bit more formally: navy blue cords, a v-neck wool sweater, a blue work shirt and a tie—this one patterned with lighthouses.

I arrived in Newport a little before one and drove straight to one of my favorite places to have lunch. The restaurant was probably the first in Oregon to be part of a bookstore. It was always jammed, both with people and stuff—everything from souvenir sweatshirts to incense burners to a great many books.

You practically have to walk sideways to get to the dining area, a comfortable, slightly funky, L-shaped room which overlooks an enclosed patio where meals are served in the summer. This is the kind of place where the waitresses always say "enjoy" when they serve your meal.

The room was only half full as I was led to a table in the corner. I sat down and the hostess handed me a menu.

"Will there be just one of you today?"

"Yes. Just me."

She picked up the place setting across from me and smiled.

"Enjoy," she said as she departed.

I looked at the menu, but I already knew what I wanted: the teriyaki chicken sandwich with homemade French fries. It was pure heaven, but messy to eat. I always had to ask for an extra napkin.

As I waited to order, I glanced at the booth in the corner and nearly choked on the water I was drinking. There sat Mr. and Mrs. Martino, big as life, along with someone whose face I couldn't quite make out. It wasn't that surprising to see university people in here. It was a favorite coastal haunt for many people I knew. It was more than a little shocking to see the objects of my soon-to-be skulking around right there in front of me.

"Shit."

"Sir. Is something wrong?"

In my intense concentration on the booth, I hadn't seen the waitress arrive. She was smiling and wearing your typical, long, flowered Sixties style dress.

"Oh no. Sorry for the language. I just remembered something I needed to do."

I ordered my meal, then looked again at the reason for my outburst. Kurt Blake, the guy with the scar and Mrs. Martino's "nephew," was the other person sitting in the booth. He might remember me from the encounter earlier in the week in the parking lot in Corvallis. I hoped Gloria wouldn't see me. She would probably recall our earlier encounter. I put on my glasses and pretended to look at the menu.

So far, they hadn't looked in my direction. He and his "aunt" and "uncle" were talking in hushed tones. They were concentrating on each other and not paying much attention to anyone else in the restaurant.

My salad arrived and I was glad to have something to do. The coach was nice-looking, like a dark, Latin lover—curly hair flecked with gray, bushy eyebrows, a long thin nose. From my meeting with her earlier, I already knew his wife was a knockout, except for all that makeup and big hair. Blake was good looking too: well-built in a body builder way, although shorter than the coach. His shaved head combined with the long scar gave him a menacing look that probably frightened dogs and small children. It sure as hell frightened me.

My main course arrived and I ate it quickly, both because I enjoyed it and because I suddenly decided I would just as soon not let the coach and members of his entourage see me. About half way through my meal, it looked as if they were getting ready to leave. The restaurant was nearly empty at this point so I knew all three of them would probably see me as they left. To eliminate that possibility, I eased into the chair opposite where I sat and pulled the silverware and my plate of food towards me. I did this when the three of them were looking at the bill, their line of sight to my table blocked, in part, by their waitress who was standing at the end of their table. Now, my back would be to them as they walked out, just another diner enjoying his chicken sandwich. I relaxed a bit, confident that I was probably invisible.

In about five minutes, I heard them putting on coats and zipping up zippers. Then, I heard their footsteps creaking on the wooden plank floor. I busied myself with the dessert menu as they passed. It took all of my willpower not to turn and look at them, I was so curious.

"... takes about fifteen minutes. . . ." The coach was speaking as they passed.

"You'll love it, Kurt darling." His wife was chiming in. Do most women call their nephews "darling", I wonder?

In several seconds, they were out of the restaurant, maybe planning to spend some time browsing in the bookstore. With more time to kill, I decided to order a piece of pecan pie for dessert.

III

Cape Foulweather is aptly named about six months of the year. As one of the highest promontories along the Oregon Coast, it is in a direct line to receive all the storms roaring in from the Pacific. There is nothing to break the force of the winds that regularly reach seventy-five miles per hour during the winter. The Cape is where Captain James Cook is reported to have first touched land in what is now Oregon in 1778. Cook didn't stay long enough to establish a settlement, but the area rates an historical marker detailing his brief visit.

Until the past few years, no one has ever lived on top of the cape, probably because of the bad weather. A development of expensive homes was now under construction, however. The bed and breakfast that Martino and his partners had purchased was an old farmhouse, long abandoned until the contractor that sold it to the coach rebuilt and modernized it.

I drove up Highway 101 and reached the top of the cape in about fifteen minutes. I turned left into a tourist parking area. I planned to leave my car here so I could move about more quietly than to announce my arrival with the noise of a car.

The road to the inn intersected with the north end of the parking lot. I parked and locked my car on the south end. To expedite a possible fast departure, I backed the car into a spot, front headed south, for a swift access to 101.

A sign stood to one side of the gate demarcating Martino's property:

CAPE FOULWEATHER INN
A bed and breakfast experience
you will never forget
Open for the season: May 1

The gate was secured by a chain and padlock threaded through an iron loop screwed into a wooden fence post. There was no way to tell if Martino and the others had gone in, but I guessed they had. I walked along the chain link fence that began at that post, heading north. The fence soon intersected with its counterpart, stretching west. The trees were so dense on the inside of the enclosure that I couldn't see anything.

I couldn't risk being seen by anyone at the inn. I looked at my watch. Three thirty. It would start getting dark in another forty-five minutes. I decided to go back to my car and wait for a while. I wanted just enough light to be able to see to get inside the fence, but not so much that I'd be obvious to anyone looking out.

I walked to my car and watched the traffic roar by on Highway 101. It was less busy than in the peak of the tourist season. There were four RVs and trucks pulling trailers. There were also a lot of log trucks, delivery trucks, and private cars. The drivers of the vehicles rarely slowed down along this stretch. That decision was probably something they regretted when southbound drivers hit the big pothole that had been carved out by winter rains just down from the crest of the hill. From my vantage point I could hear the dull thud of tires hitting the hole. A lot of cars would need to be realigned after tonight.

At about four ten, I decided the lighting was finally right for me to make my move. I got out, making sure to tuck a small penlight in my pocket and I put on my parka and a scarf.

I turned the corner and walked toward the bluff, acting like a wandering tourist in case someone challenged me. I had put the strap of my camera around my neck and put on a cap with a bill. Sunglasses seemed a bit ridiculous because we had had only rain for the past several days.

The fence ended at the edge of the cliff. The corner post was imbedded in a slab of rock which made it firm and steady—at least that is what I hoped. I took hold of the post and stepped around it so that first one foot, then the other was on the other side. Far below, the surf crashed noisily on the rocks with a force that propelled the spray up the wall almost to where I was standing. I could feel the mist on my face and taste the salt water on my lips. I had to fight the feeling of dizziness as I peered over.

When viewed from above, a small ledge was the only thing that broke the flat face of the cliff. It was about half of the way down, a bent and snaggy tree clinging to its surface. All the trees in this part of the coast were sculpted by the wind. As a consequence, they looked like they had been trimmed by hedge clippers into an aircraft carrier configuration facing east.

It was nearly dark as I set foot on the grounds of the inn. I immediately walked back along the fence so I could stay hidden in the trees. I then began to veer away from the fence and head south, still staying in the trees.

After walking a few hundred yards in that direction, I could see the back of the inn. It was a two-story wood and stone structure that seemed to have two wings. A swimming pool had been built in the corner where the two wings intersected. Wooden decking surrounded the pool, which was full of water, wafts of steam now rising from it. Floodlights shone on the pool and deck.

As I looked from the safety of the trees, a door at the rear of the house opened and Gloria Martino stepped out onto the wooden planks. She was wearing a white terry cloth robe that was so big that it engulfed her with its long sleeves and hood.

"Oh Kurt. It's so cold. I'll freeze everything off out here."

She laughed as she walked to the edge of the steaming pool. Just then, Blake came out onto the deck, wearing only a very tiny pair of swimming trunks, the better to show off his pecs and abs to his admiring audience of one.

She turned to face him and opened her robe. I knew without being able to see that the robe was all that was separating her from a case of goose bumps. He walked toward her and kissed her hard on the lips. He started fondling her breasts and she, his groin. More moaning ensued.

Where was the coach, I wondered?

Blake and Gloria then turned and jumped into the pool, the water splashing onto the wooden decking and the steam rising into the dark, cloudy sky.

As I watched their cavorting, I heard the sound of a car pulling up to the other side of the building. I stepped back carefully and walked quickly through the trees in the direction of the sound.

Floodlights bathed the front of the building in brightness so it was easy to see what was going on. A small white car had stopped in front and two young women were getting out. The front door opened and Coach Martino walked out to greet them.

". . . great . . . glad . . . see . . . both. We'll . . . have . . . time."

He kissed both women in turn and put his arms around them. The threesome moved toward the door like a flying wedge. If they didn't disengage, they would certainly knock the door off the hinges.

Did those other plans include a little *mènage à trois* sexual activity? Was the coach into group sex and wife swapping? But these girls were too young to have been married.

Sticking to the safety of the trees, I moved around the building to the area with the strongest light shining out of the windows. I could see right into what seemed to be a sitting room. A fire was burning in the fireplace and books lined two of the walls—all very elegant and cozy.

As I watched, the threesome came crashing through the door, all of them laughing. Martino started ripping off their clothes and they, in turn, began to undress him.

I couldn't watch any more. The whole thing made me sick to my stomach. I walked around to the back.

Gloria and Kurt were still in the pool, locked in a tight embrace and kissing passionately. At that moment, Kurt swam over to the edge nearest me and climbed out, and sat so his back was to me. She soon swam toward him, reaching up and tugging on his trunks. He then let her pull them off. Since Bobby Hardy was incapacitated by his steam tunnel burns, I guess Blake had become number one as the object of her affections.

"I've got a big one, just for you," he laughed.

"Nothing's too big for me," she answered, tossing her head back.

Did I want to be in the pool with her? In my mind, I took the Fifth Amendment.

I leaned forward to get a better look and then it happened. I stepped on a brittle tree limb and the sound seemed to reverberate throughout the entire forest.

"What the fuck was that?" Kurt was getting to his feet and looking in my direction.

"Don't be vulgar, darling. I didn't hear anything."

"It sounded like somebody stepped on some twig or something."

"Probably an animal, darling."

I was holding my breath and standing very still. I had the advantage, for now, because the lights around the pool area were blinding him. I decided I had better make my move.

As Kurt stepped off the deck, I moved quickly to one side, then knocked him down by sticking my foot in his way. He fell hard, the ground probably stinging his bare legs as he went down.

"What the hell?" He seemed momentarily confused by what was happening to him. I took off running back toward the ocean, figuring that I'd have a head start because of Kurt's dazed state. I found the fence easily, then began running along it toward the rear of the property.

Half way there, I stepped into a hole and the misstep sent me to my knees, pain shooting up my left leg. It felt like I had probably broken or badly wrenched my ankle.

I rolled over on my rear end and then dragged myself to the fence so I could rest and collect my thoughts a minutes. I listened for a moment or two, and heard nothing at first. So far, I seemed to be safe. I was beginning to sweat, even in the cold night air. When was I going to stop getting myself into these messes?

But then I heard the sound of someone running through the woods.

I dragged myself to my feet and limped toward the back using the fence as a support. I was almost to the end of the property and another swing around the post when I tripped again.

When I scrambled to get to my feet, however, I was not alone. I was staring into the snarling face of the biggest Doberman pinscher I had ever seen.

20

Although it growled and bared its teeth, the animal kept its distance. Maybe it was as startled to see me as I was to encounter it.

"You are basically a nice dog. Don't do anything that we'll both regret."

"Grrrr."

I stood up slowly and eased my body towards the corner of the fence and freedom.

"Grrr."

My charm offensive wasn't working. I kept my eye on the dog and kept moving. I was almost there, just a few more inches to go.

"Grrrr. Grrrr."

His growls were getting louder.

I hadn't had a dog in a few years but I remembered some basic commands.

"Stay!"

The dog ignored my command. As I swung around the fence post, it charged, catching my right shoe in its mouth as I frantically lifted my leg in the air. The dog seemed to think that he had fulfilled his guardly duties because he stepped back, dropped his prize on the ground, and looked at it. Then he took my shoe in his mouth and began to shake it. He probably hoped my foot was still in it.

His preoccupation gave me time to maneuver my body safely out of the way and make my retreat.

"Kiva. Come."

A woman's voice came from the trees. The dog stopped his shoe shaking and perked up his ears.

I scrambled down along the edge of the cliff and crouched behind a large rock. It was covered with salal and had a bent tree growing out of it. I looked down at the ledge I had seen earlier. It was way too far to reach easily. I would just have to wait and hang on here.

"Kiva. There you are. Good boy." Gloria Martino, no doubt about it.

Part of me—I won't say what part—wanted to walk up to the fence and say something like, "Hi, Gloria. Remember me? It's Tom from the other night in the parking lot. I think you've got the greatest looking body I've ever seen. Why don't you ditch the dog and the stud and run away with me?" What was happening to me?

I peered over the rock. She was carrying one of the flashlights with beams like a laser. Because she was bending over to pet the dog and walking at the same time, the flashlight's beam was erratic. It didn't illuminate enough of the scene for me.

"Drop, Kiva."

The dog had picked up my shoe and was prancing around her, proud of his trophy. She was wearing a long coat from what I could see.

"What in the hell is this?" she said loudly.

Nike, ten medium, I thought to myself.

She aimed the light toward the fence, then walked toward the corner. I ducked back down.

"Is someone there? You know you won't get very far with one shoe."

You've got that right, lady.

"Hell. It's his funeral. Right, Kiva?"

I peeked again just in time to see her turn and walk back into the trees, the dog jumping around her happily, the flashlight bobbing at her side, its rays skittering from the ground to the trees haphazardly.

Whew. That was close. I relaxed a bit and slid down so my back was resting against the rock. I knew I had to get out of here as quickly as possible. Gloria Martino would be back with reinforcements.

I decided I could probably walk if I somehow bound my ankle to give it support. I took off my scarf and wrapped it as tightly as I could around my ankle. Then I took off my left shoe and removed the laces. Next, I tied them as securely as I could over the scarf.

I stood up and steadied myself on the rock. I leaned toward the edge and hurled my remaining shoe as hard as I could out over the sea. I hoped I could do better without shoes than trying to compensate for the loss of one. Then too, I might raise fewer questions from anyone I encountered wearing no shoes than just one.

Luckily, I was wearing fairly heavy socks that protected my feet from the roots, rocks, and limbs I expected to find on the trail. I moved north through a break in the salal even though it was taking me away from the most direct route to the parking lot. I wanted to avoid running into anyone checking for me along the fence.

Just then, I spotted a tall tree limb lying on the ground. This would make a perfect crutch.

It took me about thirty minutes to reach a road. It was the old Highway 101 that ran through the small village of Otter Rock. I scrambled down a hill right near a motel. It was still early—about five fifteen—so the office was still open.

I decided to go inside to get some help. I opened the door that had one of those little bells at the top to announce arrivals.

"Good evening, sir."

A kind looking older woman looked up from a crossword puzzle.

"Do you need a room?"

"Yes, I do. But I also need some help. I had car trouble up on the highway and when I couldn't flag anyone down, I decided to walk. Then, I turned my ankle."

So far so good. She was looking at me with concern and sympathy. She leaned over and glanced down at my feet.

"What happened to your shoes?"

"Yes, my shoes . . . I decided I'd make better time if I took them off. I mean the one was hurting like he . . . heck. And when I fell, I lost them."

"Both of them? You lost your shoes?" Her face was registering a mild look of disapproval as if she couldn't imagine anyone losing his shoes.

"Yeah. As you can see, I'm in a real bad way. If I take a room, is there anyone who could drive me up to my car? I mean to get my bag?"

"Carl?" She had turned her head to the rear and was yelling towards an open door. I could hear a TV set in the distance.

"Carl's my husband. He's a bit deaf but he's a good driver. He'll take you to your car. Just fill out this card and I'll go get him. Carl!"

She smiled and disappeared through the door.

I filled in the typical motel registration card, deciding to pay in cash in case someone checked later. I was becoming paranoid. I got out my wallet to get my driver's license number and to have my cash handy.

Just then, the owner and her husband came through the door from the back.

"This is Carl, my husband."

A man who looked a lot like the comedian Jonathan Winters stepped forward and shook my hand.

"Tom Martin." My new alias.

He smiled and pumped my hand vigorously. He was wearing bib overalls and a fishing hat.

"I forgot my manners. I'm Gladys. Gladys Summers."

"My pleasure, ma'am."

Gallantry was not dead after all. I executed a little bow and put on a big smile. I wanted her to remember "that nice young man" who rented a room, if anybody asked later.

"So ye got some car trouble?"

"Yes, it died on me up on the highway. It's in the parking lot of the rest area on top of Cape Foulweather. I've got some extra shoes in there."

"I know that place. Will ye want to be goin' there now?"

"Yes, I would. I'd hate to have anything happen to my car. Here's my registration card. I'll pay in cash. What was the cost for one night?"

She told me and I quickly paid.

"Here's the key to number four, Mr . . . " She looked at the card.

". . . Martin. We're glad to have you. It's lucky you got us. We're closing tomorrow night for a month. We always spend the month of February at our daughter's mobile home in Yuma."

"Boy, that was lucky for me."

Carl and I headed for the door. I turned around for one last smile. It was getting easier to walk in my stocking feet.

"Thanks for your help. You saved my life!"

I followed Carl to an old pickup truck parked next to the building. He unlocked the door on the passenger side and I got in. He walked around and got in.

"Got a bum leg?"

"I twisted my ankle, then lost my shoes in all the confusion."

"What kind of confusion was that?"

He looked somewhat skeptical that anyone in his right mind could possibly lose his shoes. He started the engine and began to back out.

"I mean my falling and all."

"Oh yes, I . . . see." He didn't seem convinced. He pulled the truck out onto the road and turned left. We were soon driving up the steep incline that would take us to 101.

"You're not from these parts."

"No. I live in Corvallis."

"Oh, you're with the college then?"

"Yes. I teach at Oregon University."

"In my time it was OAC. The AC was for agricultural college."

"You went there, Mr. Summers?"

"Oh no. I had to go to work to support my mama. My younger brother did, though. He became a doctor. Didn't see too much of him most of the time after we grew up. He lived in Seattle. He's dead now."

"I'm sorry."

"Don't be. That highfalutin son of a bitch always thought he was better than me."

We had reached Highway 101 by this time and he was waiting for a break in the traffic to turn south. I hoped we could sail right into the lot and I could get my car without anyone from the Cape Foulweather Inn seeing me.

The parking lot was deserted.

"Is this it?"

"Yeah. There it is. Safe and sound." I got into my car and, predictably, it started immediately.

"I really appreciate your help," I shouted, waving off any questions of car trouble. "I want you to have this for your trouble." I reached into my shirt pocket and retrieved a $20 bill I had stashed there earlier for precisely this purpose.

"It'll be our secret." I winked at him. Gladys looked to me like someone who handled the money. Then we headed for the motel.

21

SUNDAY

The morning dawned cold and rainy, making it an ideal day to tend to my bad ankle and get back to Corvallis. I had bought some salve and an elastic bandage at a convenience store in Depoe Bay the night before. The combination of treatments seemed to work wonders because I could put weight on the bad leg without a lot of pain.

I allowed myself the luxury of sleeping in, excusing the laggardness by both my injury and the need to get ready for the busy week ahead. After I showered and dressed, I packed up quickly and walked over to the office to check out.

As it had the night before, the little bell on the door roused Gladys Summers from her crossword puzzle. She got up when she saw me and walked over to the desk.

"Morning, Mr. Martin. Did we sleep well and are we feeling better?"

"Sure did. Thanks."

"Carl. Carl."

I jumped at her bellow toward the back of the room, where I could hear the TV. It sounded like a basketball game was on.

"He wanted to see you again and tell you about something. I see you're able to walk without limping. That's good."

"Yes, I put some salve on my ankle and bound the whole thing tight with an Ace bandage."

"Oh, good morning, young fella."

"Hello, Carl. How are you today?"

Gladys pushed him forward as if to jog his memory.

"Go on, Carl. Tell him what happened."

The old man thought for a minute, then seemed to recollect what it was he was supposed to remember.

"Some men came looking for ye earlier today. Gladys and I, we played dumb and didn't tell them a thing."

"Who were they? Did you recognize them?"

"A friendly guy who did the talking and a youngster who looked mean and had a lot of muscles."

"What did you tell them."

This time Gladys spoke up, her eyes shining brightly.

"I kept them busy in here while Carl went out and closed the doors to the garage where your car is. I mean so they'd think we didn't have any guests. I told them we were closed for the season which, as of today, we are. We're leaving for Yuma this afternoon, soon as I do up your room."

"We just hoped you wouldn't come strolling out whilst they were here," he added.

I smiled at them both and shook their hands. "I can't begin to thank you. You save me from a lot of hassles, believe me."

Gladys leaned toward me and spoke in a loud whisper.

"Son, are you in bad trouble? We can loan you some money if you need to get over the border or anything like that."

"Oh, no. It's nothing like that. Those men aren't the police. They think I saw something I shouldn't have seen."

A quizzical look came over her face. As someone who had heard and, no doubt, passed on a lot of gossip in her time, she really wanted to hear the juicy details. I hated to disappoint her. "Gladys. Carl."

They were both looking at me intently.

"For your own good. I don't think I should tell you any more. Let me say that it's nothing against the law and it's nothing you two will get into trouble about. Okay?"

They nodded their heads in unison. She stepped forward and grabbed my hand with both of hers.

"If you need us, we're always here for you, son."

"How can we be here for him if we're in Yuma? That makes no sense, Glad."

"Oh, Carl. It's a figure of speech!"

"Thanks. That means a lot to me. Thanks for everything. Do I owe any more on my bill?"

"No. You paid me last night."

I reached for my wallet and extracted two twenty dollar bills. "Take this for your trip. A little gift from me. Have a nice dinner somewhere on me."

"Oh, you don't need to . . ."

Carl started to speak but Gladys cut him off. She grabbed the money and put it in the pocket of her smock.

22

MONDAY

A colleague substituted for me in my one class the next day so I could concentrate on working with Joel Friedkin and his film crew. I dreaded the thought of hobbling through the week on my bum ankle but didn't really think I had much choice.

I had decided the night before that I hadn't broken any bones or even sprained it. There was no swelling or discoloration. Probably just a bad strain.

I met Joel at eight the next morning in The Commons, the large eating area in the student union building.

"You look terrible, Tom. Are you limping? What happened?"

"I went hiking over on the coast this weekend and turned my ankle. It's nothing serious. I'll be fine."

"I won't worry then. What have you got for me today?"

"In the first place, good weather." I looked out of the tall window next to where we were seated.

"Yeah. A miracle in Oregon in late January. What else?"

"I've got clearances for all the filming you want—both outside and inside some classrooms."

I handed him a neatly typed list of times and locations, plus a map of campus.

"I'll be with you most of today and tomorrow but this will serve as a backup in case I'm not around."

"What else?"

"I've arranged for security. And, most important of all, I've got you two new principal actors. They've been working with the drama teacher and they're ready to go."

"Good. You're hired."

He smiled and chuckled at his own joke. Joel was someone who rarely allowed humor to interfere with his day, especially if it displaced his usual form of communication: anger and abruptness.

We went over the schedule in greater detail and drank our coffee. Several times, I got up and hobbled over to get refills. At about eight forty-five, I looked up to see our two new stars walking in the end door. I stood up and waved.

Sara Nyland and Sam Murphy looked like archetype college students: clean-cut, good looking, squeaky clean—and, to Skip Olson's probable relief, white. I left the choice of actors to my friend, the drama professor. I hadn't mentioned that race mattered. Although I thought the use of Del Johnson in the video sent the kind of message I wanted the university to convey, the current circumstances dictated that we go with whomever we could get. I would have to deal with the politically correct aspects of the situation later. For now, these kids would do fine. Because they were both aspiring actors, their appearances in these TV ads would, no doubt, be very welcome additions to their demo reels.

"Sara. Sam. Good morning."

I stood up.

"Gol. What happened to you, Professor Martindale?"

Being from California, Sara usually sounded more spacey than she probably was. She did, in fact, have a 3.78 grade point average in her major, Speech.

"No one who works for me ever utters the word, 'gol.'"

Joel had not looked up from the pages in front of him. He had apparently decided to give poor Sara an immediate baptism of fire. She looked horrified.

"In the first place, I doubt it is a word." He looked at them both.

"Walk over there and turn around. Both of you."

They looked at each other, then followed his directions to walk away from the table a few steps, then turn around.

"Okay, now back toward me."

Joel was directing and didn't care that others in the large room were looking up from their newspapers and breakfasts to stare.

"Screw them. Look only at me. Smile. Frown. Hold your faces impassive."

Sam complied quickly, but Sara was having trouble with the last instruction.

"Jesus Christ! Impassive! That means no expression."

She seemed about to burst into tears but managed to control her emotions and to follow his directions.

"Good. Come over here and sit down."

They did that and soon joined us at the table.

"You need to get used to me shouting at you and being blunt. I'm after one thing here: a quality production. You do what I tell you to do and we'll achieve that. If you fail to listen, I'll get mad and yell at you. It's really very simple. Okay?

They both nodded, Sam looking more convinced than Sara.

"You've got your scripts memorized. Am I right?"

They nodded again.

"We should be in business then. Let's get out of here and get you guys into a little makeup."

We stood as a group and began walking toward the end door. I fell to the rear because of my ankle. As I got to the door, I noticed Chuck Gates, the U of O public affairs guy, sitting at another table. I hobbled over.

"Slumming with the Aggies, Gates?

"My, aren't we testy this morning, Martindale?"

"It always ruins my day to see industrial spies before lunch."

"Is that what you think I'm doing? I came up here to use the library."

"Boy, what a crock that is! In the interest of fairness, I'd like you to leave campus. I've been content to wait for the U of O ad to appear on my TV screen, you need to do the same for our efforts."

"What do I say here, something about it being a free country and all that? Last time I checked, this university was public and everything in it owned by taxpayers like me."

I leaned down and placed my face close to his. "I think we'll need to make an exception in this case, Gates."

He spread his arms and extended the palms of his hands in a kind of "I surrender" gesture. I turned and walked out the door.

The Quad in front of the student union building was being rapidly transformed into a movie set. A large motor home was parked on the street to the west. It housed Joel's office, a small editing bay, even wardrobe areas and makeup chairs. The sign on its side heralded both the name of his company and his inflated pretensions: Imperial Productions.

I climbed up the step and into the entryway of the motor home.

"Hi, Tom. Good to see you again."

It was Patsy, Joel Friedkin's assistant.

"Where's the great man?"

"He took the kids in the back for makeup. Boy, they are something. Really look the part. Are they for real? I mean no zits or anything."

"We grow them wholesome and handsome down here on the farm, Patsy. You got a phone I can use?"

"Sure. Here's my cell. Step into Joel's office for privacy."

I opened a door and stepped up into a small but beautifully furnished room. Inside, you'd never know you were in a motor home. I sat down at Joel's desk and used the phone. I knew the number by heart.

"Hadley Collins."

"It's Tom Martindale. Good morning."

"Oh Tom, good to hear from you. Are you on the job so early?"

"Yeah. The director and his crew are here. We're about to start two days of shooting on campus."

"I remembered. It's on my calendar. I plan to walk over later and look in on things."

"Good, I think you should. But that's not why I called. I was just in The Commons with Joel Friedkin, the director. I ran into that creep from the U of O I told you about–Charles Gates."

"And?"

"We chatted and he made it clear that he was going to hang around and watch us shoot. I don't want him to know anything about our strategy. I doubt that he'd copy it. They don't need to, their campaign is good. But it gripes me that he's even around."

"Aren't you being a bit paranoid, Tom?"

"More than a bit. I'm paranoid about everything. Didn't my analyst call you?"

She chuckled. "Yeah. I know what you mean. This guy does seem a bit too zealous. Let me see if I can shake him up a bit. You'll hear from me later. Just go ahead with your routine. I'll see you soon."

"Can you tell me what to expect?"

"Just trust me on this, Tom. Wait and be surprised."

"Thanks, Hadley."

The door to the back opened and Joel walked in. "God, Tom! You startled me!"

"Sorry. I was just borrowing your phone to call my boss. That Chuck Gates from the U of O is around. He's spying on us, trying to get an idea of what we're doing."

"That guy's got a lot of balls to come on this campus and hang out. And he knows we know who he is!"

"My boss Hadley's going to try to do something. Let's go on about our routine. I'll keep an eye on him for now. Are the kids ready?"

"I think the girl may be a bit of a bimbo, but she looks good."

"That's all that counts in this case, I guess. She doesn't have to be a Rhodes Scholar."

"Roads scholar? She's an engineering major?"

"No, not exactly."

"Yeah, yeah, whatever."

"How are we doing on time?"

He looked at his watch. "Five to nine. We'd better get ready to rock and roll."

We both stood up and walked out of the motor home and onto the street. The nice day and the hum of the generators powering all the equipment had attracted a small but growing crowd. Everyone was being kept back by tape that looked just like what police use to cordon off a crime scene.

The two student actors were standing to one side of the front of the student union. Joel was talking to them as a makeup woman made last minute changes.

For the time being, I kept my distance and scanned the crowd for Gates. He had positioned himself under a tree just back of the nearest tape line. When he saw me looking at him, he smiled and bowed slightly.

Arrogant bastard. I glared and turned my head back to the action. Joel had finished his instructions and had stepped out to an area to the side of the camera. He nodded to his assistant, Patsy, who put an electronic megaphone to her mouth.

"Good morning, everyone. We're happy to see all you Beavers out here today."

"Yeaaaaa!"

The crowd yelled and whooped with a scattering of applause.

"Go Beavs!"

A loud male voice rang out from the pack.

"That's right. We want the Beavers to succeed so we're making some ads to run on television."

"Yeaaaa!"

"Right. Some of the ads will be shot outside—like here in front of your beautiful memorial building."

"MU!" said a voice from the crowd."

"What?" Patsy was perplexed.

The same voice replied. "It's called the MU—for Memorial Union."

"Oh, of course. Sorry. Anyway, we're going to take advantage of the good weather and shoot outdoors here and in a few other parts of campus. Then we'll do some filming inside later in the week. At any rate, we hope you enjoy watching us. All we ask is that you be quiet when we're shooting to keep out the background noise. Do that and we'll keep on schedule. And we'll keep my boss, Joel Friedkin here, happy."

As she said that, Friedkin turned around to face the crowd. He took off his cap and bowed toward the crowd in an exaggerated manner.

"Yeaaaa! Yeaaaa!"

Then he turned to the actors and nodded again. The bright lights lining the perimeter of the area to be filmed came on. A sound man extended a microphone toward the two students.

Patsy faced the crowd and brought her arms down, her hands extended palms down as if she were trying to tamp out a fire. The group became quiet very quickly.

"Quiet on the set. Camera one roll and we'll have action."

Now Joel had the electronic megaphone.

The two students started to stroll side-by-side across the front of the majestic building.

". . . and you know, Sara, some of my classes are taught by senior professors. I mean they don't turn them over to graduate students."

"Gol, Sam. That prol-ly wouldn't . . ."

"Cut!"

Joel looked somewhat irritated but remained in control of himself—for now. He walked toward the two, who looked terrified. I walked into the magic enclosure to step in if necessary. Joel was doing one of his famous stage whispers, during which every word sounded like a hiss. What he said had no relationship to the smile on his face, which was apparently for the benefit of the crowd.

"You need to e-nun-ci-ate, Sally."

"It's Sara," I added helpfully.

"Sara, Sally, whatever. It doesn't matter if she can't say her lines properly."

He smiled at the now frightened young woman. "You can't say 'gol.' It isn't in the script. And the word I want is 'prob-ab-ly' not 'prol-ly.' Say 'I know, Sam' or 'That's right, Sam,' not 'gol.' Okay? Got that?

She nodded her head.

"No tears now. This is the big time now, not class. We're playing for keeps here, with a lot riding on what we do. Do you understand?"

She nodded again.

"Good. I'm glad we're clear . . . makeup!"

He was yelling over his shoulder to the woman in charge of keeping faces properly prepared for the harsh eye of the camera. The woman dashed in and went to work.

"Don't get upset, dear. He's just doing this for your own good. Give me a nice smile. There we are, dear. Just relax," she said softly.

The woman seemed to calm Sara. I didn't say anything. I stepped back to the sidelines to resume my vigil.

Gates was still standing by the tree. When he saw me looking at him, he gave me a small salute along with a smug look that seemed to say, "This wouldn't happen with our ads at the great U of O." I turned away in disgust. This guy was getting on my nerves. Every once in a while, he would cough and sneeze. I hoped that behavior was not a preview of what he would do when the cameras were rolling again.

The two kids resumed their stroll on the walkway in front of the MU.

". . . and you know, Sara, some of my classes are taught by senior professors. I mean they don't turn them over to graduate students."

"I've heard that, Sam. That's impressive. That prob-ab-ly wouldn't happen in most large universities."

They glided by the camera, which swung around to record them as they passed. The scene was perfect.

Just then, the day got decidedly better. Hadley Collins was making her way to the front of the crowd accompanied by one of the tallest state troopers I had ever seen. She looked at me quizzically, then at Gates who was so busy blowing his nose that he hadn't noticed her yet. I nodded in his direction and she smiled.

She whispered something to the trooper and started walking over to me. The trooper moved toward Gates, who saw him coming and looked alarmed. The big man didn't say anything to Gates, who was, after all, on public property.

Gates walked along the tape to find another vantage point. The policeman followed him, never saying anything to him or even looking at him.

Gates moved again and the trooper followed, always looking straight ahead stoically.

Before long, the savvy crowd caught on to what was taking place and started to cheer every time the trooper took up his position next to the increasingly frustrated Gates.

Hadley Collins had joined me by this time.

"That ought to fix the son of a bitch," she whispered.

I looked at Gates again and saw that he was walking right towards us.

"Chuck Gates, U of O advertising genius extraordinaire meet Hadley Col . . ."

"Shut up, you bastard. This isn't over. I won't be harassed like this."

Hadley stepped up to him before I could say anything.

"Look, you little jerk. I went to college with Nan Browning, you know, the wife of your boss, the president of the University of Oregon. I know she'd be glad to pass along the details of your little spying episode today, I mean pass them along to her husband. It won't be official, but it could cause you some grief down the line."

"I don't know what you're talking about," sputtered Gates. "Last time I looked, it wasn't against the law to stand in a crowd on a college campus."

"It isn't that, Gates," I added. "It's hanging around the studio in Portland, talking to a girl who was later found murdered."

Gates' face got very pale. Even Hadley shot me a quizzical look. Where was I going with this? I wasn't sure but I just wanted to get this guy out of my face any way I could.

"This isn't the end of this, Martindale."

I stood toe to toe with him, matching his glare.

"Oh, I'm really shaking in my boots."

He turned and walked off.

"We made short work of him, didn't we, Tom?" Hadley was smiling.

"Yeah we did. He won't be showing his smug face around here anytime soon. I don't think he saw enough to help him. He can only guess at what we're planning."

"What was that you said about him talking to Emily Morgan?"

"I'll tell you later. I was just trying to scare him."

She turned to signal the state trooper with a thumbs up sign. He smiled at the two of us and walked back into the crowd.

"Yeaaaa! Yeaaaa!"

The kids were cheering him as he made his way among them. Odd how quickly people take sides in the little sidebar dramas that come up every day.

"Thanks, Hadley. You defused that situation nicely."

"Any time, Tom. That wasn't an idle threat about calling Nan Browning. I really did go to college with her. I won't do anything just yet. Let's see what Gates does. I hope this will cause him to back off, but if he doesn't . . ."

She winked.

"I agree. He hasn't seen enough to really know what we're doing. As long as he doesn't get a hold of a script, we're still secure. He wouldn't be here if he had that. I'll talk to Joel about security again. We'll be all right."

"I'm supposed to be in two meetings. I've got to get back to my office."

"Thanks again, Hadley. I'll see you soon."

After the diversion of the dust-up over Gates, Joel resumed shooting the same scene. He was apparently satisfied with it, but wanted to have a choice of takes just in case. Sara was gaining more confidence each time she said her lines. Sam had been that way all along.

"Cut. That's good. We've got a keeper here. Take five, everyone."

All the people involved in the production visibly relaxed knowing this particular scene was complete. Patsy moved forward to lead Sara and Sam back to the motor home to rest. Other technicians began to disassemble lighting setups and put the cameras back in their carrying cases. Everything would now be moving inside to the department's photo studio where the shots Emily and Del had done in Portland would be redone. The crowd started to disperse.

"A good morning's work, Joel, don't you think?"

The director was looking pleased with himself as he crossed things off a list he had attached to a clipboard.

"Yeah, right. Very good. Better than I thought. That chick's still kind of spacey, but we can live with that. I just can't give her any leeway. The other girl, the one who died . . ."

"Emily."

"Yeah, Emily. She was a quick study and had the right instincts. This one's a real valley girl with all her 'prol-lies' and 'gols.' Jesus! What an airhead!"

"So I'll take you into the studio whenever you're ready. It's in that huge building over there."

"Ag Hall, eh? Will there be manure on the floors? Heh, heh."

"I won't dignify that with a response, Joel."

"Sorry. You're awfully touchy this morning."

"Listen, I want you to watch out for that guy from the U of O, Chuck Gates. It really bothers me that he was here watching you perform your magic act. He says he was just checking out the opposition, but it really frosts me. He was the guy involved in that incident with the state trooper a few minutes ago."

"That's who that was. He looked vaguely familiar. I was just concentrating on re-shooting. I didn't really fix on his face."

"Well, he left in a huff but made all kinds of threats about this not being the end of it and stuff like that. I think he'll still try to get a hold of the script. How many copies are there?"

"Just three, all numbered and held close. I have one, you have one, and Patsy, my assistant, has the third. Everyone else has read it, but they get only the sections we're working on. Then they turn them back to Patsy. I'll give everybody another lecture on security tonight."

"Good idea."

"It's eleven. Maybe we can get the motor home and van moved and you can show me what the facilities are before lunch. Let's go tell Patsy."

Just as we got to the motor home, Sara and Sam stepped out. They saw me and waved. Sara, however, continued to wave even after I had returned the gesture. She was looking at someone behind me. I turned and my heart skipped a beat. Coming towards us from the center of the Quad was Kurt Blake and two young women, one on each arm.

"Shannon! Tiffanie! Over here," Sara shouted.

When I got a good look at the faces of the women with Blake, I wanted to be somewhere else. Shannon and Tiffanie were the two women I had seen cavorting with Coach Martino on Cape Foulweather.

Joel went into his traveling office, but I stayed where I was, my curiosity overcoming any urge to flee.

"Gol, you guys. You missed me. I'm a star."

Sara was absolutely giddy about her debut as a commercial actress.

The threesome stopped in front of us. The two girls hugged Sara, kissing the air or her hair in the process. They were very pretty in an overly-made-up, slightly plastic way. They had great figures too, a fact I could attest to from my earlier observations.

"You guys. This is my favorite professor, Mr. Martindale. Shannon, Tiffanie."

"Hi. How are you doing?"

We shook hands. They had no flicker of recognition.

"It's totally awesome to meet you," one of them said. I didn't know which was which.

With Kurt Blake, however, it was another story. He seemed to be trying to place my face. Never mind that he had been trying to displace my face two days ago.

"This is Kurt Blake, their . . . uh . . . friend."

At that, all three young women broke into gales of laughter.

"How's it goin', man."

Blake's handshake was firm and he put pressure on my fingers a bit longer than necessary.

"Have we met?"

"No, I don't think so. I never forget the face of someone I've had in class. You're a student here? Right?"

"No, I dropped out a few years ago. I'm in business with my aunt and uncle."

"His aunt is Mrs. Martino, the wife of the assistant football coach," Sara said.

"Are you doing something with the team?"

"Nothing like that. We're partners in a bed and breakfast over on the coast."

"Oh, I see. I bet you do well in the summer."

"Not sure yet. This'll be our first one coming up."

"And you two—are you in business or do you go here too?"

All three girls broke into laughter again, the fake, sidesplitting kind that never seems sincere.

"We go here," said Shannon as she tried to regain her composure.

"We're all in the same sorority," Tiffanie added.

"They used to be on the rally squad but now they're doing . . ."

Sara looked at them for guidance.

"Special projects."

Those words sent them back into a high state of hilarity. Blake shot them a look that ended their laughter immediately. I made an elaborate gesture of looking at my watch.

"Boy, I'm late. I've got to get going."

I turned to the three and shook hands again.

"Great to meet you.

| | |

In the next hour, I helped Joel and his crew move the motor home and the accompanying van and all their equipment to a parking spot on the street next to Ag Hall, then headed up to the photo studio on the second floor.

"I think my pass key will work."

The lock turned easily and I opened the door for Joel, turning on the lights as I stepped in.

"Not bad. It will be a bit cramped, but it'll do nicely," Joel said.

"Glad you're pleased. This used to be a classroom until last year when my colleagues who teach photography raised the money to install the lights and various backdrops."

Joel walked around the room. "Nice job. I'm impressed. Okay, Marty. Let's set up lights here and here. Where's Patsy?"

"Here, boss." She pushed her way through the others.

"Makeup can be over there on that old wooden table, wardrobe over there behind the backdrop. It'll do just fine. Okay, people. Let's get ready, then we'll break for lunch."

He turned to me. "Where can the caterers set up?"

"How about my outer office? It's a conference room with tables and chairs."

"Show it to Patsy."

The two of us left the others and walked down the hall and through the fire doors to my office. She went to make arrangements with the catering company. As I had learned last week in Portland, film people eat very well when they're working.

I sat down at my desk and checked my messages. Then, acting on an idea that had been forming in my mind for several days, I called the editor of the student newspaper. He was one of our best journalism students, always eager to delve into a good story.

Jack Jennings picked up his phone after one ring.

"Hi, Jack. Tom Martindale."

"Professor Martindale. If you're calling about that paper from last term . . ."

"No, no. Nothing like that. I've got a story I think you're going to love."

23

The old oak table in my conference room was piled with food. The caterers had outdone themselves with ham, turkey, beef, six kinds of salad, three kinds of quiche, and various cakes, pies, and cookies. Coolers held all kinds of soft drinks and bottled water packed in ice. Of course, the university was paying for this, so I planned to eat a lot.

After we filled our china plates, we went the hall to the large studio room where the filming would resume in about an hour. Everyone was in a good mood, including Joel, who was almost jaunty, a frame of mind I'd never seen him in before. He was usually so uptight and petulant. We were sitting together on the floor, our backs against the wall.

"I think we're actually going to finish this sucker ahead of schedule," Joel said between bites of quiche. "If things go well this afternoon, we can finish our outdoor stuff tomorrow, providing the weather holds . . . Patsy!"

He turned his head to yell at his long-suffering assistant, who was standing near the door, balancing her plate and a cup. She hurried over.

"Yes, boss?"

"What's the weather forecast for tomorrow?"

"Cold and clear last time I checked. No more weather fronts due until day after tomorrow!"

"Good news! Great. Thanks, Pats."

He turned back to me, suddenly ready to ignore her now that his question had been answered.

"Won't you join us?" I asked, looking up at her.

"No, no. Pats always has too much to do to sit still for very long. Am I right?"

"No, no. I insist."

I got up and took her plate and cup and put them down on the floor next to me. I sat down and patted the floor.

"You look like you could use a sit-down lunch," I said, looking up at her.

She laughed, a look of relief on her face. Friedkin kept eating, apparently not caring whether she joined us or disappeared altogether.

"How long have you been in the film business, Patsy?" I asked.

"Ten years," she replied, sitting down next to me. "I started in L.A., then moved up here to take care of my mother after my father died. I went to work for Joel soon after."

We talked for ten minutes or so about teaching and journalism and how we thought the filming was going. Suddenly, Friedkin could take it no longer.

"Don't you have a hundred things to do to get ready for this afternoon, Pats?"

She looked at him with a mixture of contempt and anger.

"Right, boss. The world would probably end if I rested for too long," she said as she got up and left, giving me a limp smile over her shoulder.

"Now what brought that on?" Joel seemed genuinely puzzled by her anger.

Joel went back to his lunch and we finished in silence.

"So we complete outdoor shooting tomorrow. You've got all that footage of animals and stock exchanges and fashion shows rolling into my studio. Clearances too?"

I nodded and placed my plate on the floor. "I've got lists in my office."

"Good. I thought so. You do good work, Tom. So I get all of this mess in my editing room in Portland, maybe get these kids to come up and record some voice-over stuff and, presto, we're done."

"How long do you think, realistically?"

"Before we're ready for air?"

I nodded my head in the affirmative, nibbling on a cookie.

"Two weeks or so. You can expect to drop these cassettes off at the TV station by February twentieth."

"That's about what we planned. It's a little late to get to kids who already have made commitments for next fall, but we'll at least show the university flag and catch some late deciders."

"Late! Good God, it's barely February!"

"We do everything ahead of time in the academic world. Things that take weeks outside in the real world take months or even years at the university."

"I'd go bankrupt if I ran my business that way."

"I know what you mean. Look, Joel. I've got some errands to run this afternoon for an hour or so."

"Don't worry. We'll be fine on our own."

Joel got up and, as if some signal had been given, the room suddenly came to life. Patsy and all the technicians gulped down the last remnants of their lunches, then stacked their plates on a small table.

In five minutes, the room had turned back into its studio mode. Technicians were arranging lights and checking sound levels. Joel moved Sara and Sam onto the set and was talking to them earnestly. I ducked out the door to walk to my meeting with Jack Jennings.

III

The Commons had been the gathering place for students since the 1940s. You got your food on one side, paid for it, then moved out into the larger room presided over by a hideous wooden carving of the college mascot, Benny Beaver. It was a good place to study, socialize, or hold an informal meeting.

Jack Jennings was already seated at one of the tables by the windows when I got there. He was an older than average student who had come to journalism after several years as a logger. He had discovered his love for writing and reporting later than most students and was trying to make up for lost time. He excelled at both activities and was fearless when it came to going after a story.

"Jack. How you doing? I've missed having you in a class this term."

"Yeah, Professor Martindale. I've missed being in one of your classes too. I plan to take that seminar in critical reviewing next term, though. That should be cool."

"It usually is. Lots of writing, but of short pieces. You know, reviews of books, movies, TV, plays, even restaurants."

"I can't wait. I'll get that paper to you soon to take care of my incomplete."

He sipped his coffee.

"I guess it's up to me to say something like, 'You probably wonder why I called you here'?"

He laughed. "Something like that. You said something about a story I'm going to love."

"Yeah. Where to begin?"

I sipped a soft drink and looked around to see who was sitting nearby.

"What I'm going to tell you didn't come from me. If I'm connected to this, I could get in real trouble and other people could be hurt. I trust you to protect me."

"Whew. That sounds pretty heavy! I can see the awards for my investigative reporting rolling in already. Sure. We've been friends a long time. You've helped me become what I am today. I won't betray you. Count on me."

We shook hands on it and I believed him.

"Thanks for the compliment, Jack. I wouldn't trust this stuff with just anyone."

I drank more of my soft drink.

"Let me give you your lead first, then fill in the details later. There are two prongs to the story: the athletic department is not giving its black athletes a fair shake. I mean they're dropping them after their eligibility runs out if they can't cut it academically."

"That goes on everywhere, but I hadn't heard about it happening here. It really sucks."

"Well, it is happening. You can go at it by using the national stuff in a sidebar or something. The kid to talk to is a player named Gabriel Washington. Officially, I don't know who to suggest. The head academic adviser down there, Duke Ramsay, is dead."

"Yeah, everybody's talking about it but the police. They aren't saying a thing but I assume he was murdered. Any connection to this story?"

"There might be a link between his death and the other angle I want to tell you about. There may be something sexual going on between the assistant coach Ricky Martino and cheerleaders, and his wife and some of the players."

"Wow! I can't believe it! How awesome! Pulitzer Prize, here I come!"

"You see why this whole thing is sensitive. I'm not even sure how to suggest you tackle that part of the story. I guess I'd go first to the rally squad, then to some of the players."

"My girlfriend used to have a roommate who's now a rally girl—or whatever you call them."

"Rally person," I volunteered.

We both laughed.

"This is sensitive for another reason. One of the former tutors for the football team was Emily Morgan, a student and advisee of mine."

"I knew Emily. I had her in several classes. Is her death mixed up with this?"

"I'm not sure. Also, the police are looking for another student I know in connection with her death. Delroy Johnson. He's on the team too. The two of them were friends. I'm trying to help him and find out who killed her."

"Can you get me an interview with him? Do you know where he is?"

"I can't help you with that. I don't think he did anything wrong, just like the time last year when I vouched for you after that Psych professor accused you of plagiarism."

"Yeah, wasn't that a crock of you-know-what? You really saved my ass on that one."

"A friend of mine is the head of the state police unit on campus, but I can't get her help because she considers me someone who knows more than I'm telling. I've been putting off making an official statement. That's why I called you. One thing, though: you can't publish anything until it's all over. It's too dangerous. You'll get your exclusive then and maybe the truth will come out."

"I can't wait to get started." He looked at his watch. "I've got a class, then a staff meeting. I'm sorry, but I gotta split."

"Remember. Mum's the word."

"My lips are sealed."

He walked away with a big smile on his face. There's nothing like the prospect of investigating a big story to get a reporter's adrenaline pumping. Glancing around the room, I saw a familiar face.

Kurt Blake was sitting three tables away. When he saw me recognize him, he raised his coffee cup in mock salute, a big grin on his face.

24

When I got back to the office, April Greer, Emily's roommate, was sitting on the floor outside my door. It was something students did a lot because there were no benches in the halls. The door to my office was closed, and the lights out, which meant that the caterers had finished cleaning up.

"Hi, April. How are you feeling?"

I hadn't seen her around the department since she told me about her friend's death the week before.

"Oh hi, Mr. Martindale. I'm doin' all right. I just wanted to talk to you."

"Sure. Come in."

I opened the door and turned on the light. The conference room was neat as the proverbial pin. The caterers had not only taken every scrap of leftover food and dirty plates and utensils with them, they had even mopped and polished the floor.

"Sit down, please. What can I do for you?"

"I went home for Emily's memorial service. You knew her family had a private service."

"Yeah, I found that out. I sent flowers. I hope they got there."

"Yes, they did. Her dad had me go over the cards with him and identify everyone I knew from the university. I told him who you were and how much Emily looked up to you."

She had been on the verge of tears since she sat down, but now they flowed freely down her cheeks.

"Here, April. Take my handkerchief."

"Thanks." She dabbed at her eyes and that seemed to break the tension.

"I think I'm okay, then I lose it again. It just seems so unfair, what happened to Em, I mean."

"Yeah. I feel the same way. So who else sent flowers?"

"The sorority and the dean of students office and Del Johnson."

"Del sent flowers? I thought he was in hiding."

"I guess so, but he sent them from somewhere."

"What did her dad think of that? She told me he didn't approve of their relationship."

"He didn't and still feels the same way, but he didn't say much about it when we went over the cards. I think he's kinda numb right now. But there's one card he wanted me to ask you about."

She put her large book bag on the table and began to rummage through it. She unzipped compartment after compartment before finding what she was looking for.

"This must be it."

The card said "With Deepest Sympathy" at the top and had an angel on the left side.

I read the inscription aloud: "For all that might have been, your Grizzly."

"Have you ever heard of someone named Grizzly? I sure haven't."

"No. It doesn't ring any bells with me. Of course it's a nickname but it conjures up images of some kind of rugged, outdoorsy guy. Also, it seems like a name an older person might use. I mean, there used to be a TV character called Grizzly Adams."

She looked blank. "Really? On MTV?"

I laughed. "It was on one of the networks in the 1970s. It was for kids. Anyway, her father thought I'd know?"

"He hoped it might ring a bell. He wanted to send a thank you for the beautiful flowers. I don't think he was thinking beyond that, I mean to think anything romantic might be going on between Em and anybody. You know, it was a 'daddy's little girl' kind of thing. My dad's the same way with me."

"I don't blame him."

I turned the card over in my hand as if some kind of clue might be hidden on the back.

"The flowers were wired to Medford, so the person who sent them can't be identified by handwriting."

"Yeah, I guess. I didn't call the florist but there wouldn't be any reason for someone to physically bring the flowers clear down there. And besides, they came from a shop down there."

"Did Emily ever mention other guys to you, I mean guys she was dating beside Del?"

"I knew all about the situation with Del. That was really rough on both of them. I don't think he had anything to do with her death, do you?"

"There is no way he could have been involved. I'd stake my career on that. How about anyone else—like any older guys?"

"She said an important university official had a crush on her, but she wouldn't tell me who it was."

"Maybe a coach?"

"I don't know. She told me once about this older guy who really liked her and gave her gifts and . . ."

April's face turned a deep crimson.

"Had sex with her?

She laughed. "Yeah, he wanted to get her into bed, but she wouldn't do it. She had broken up with Del but I think she still loved him."

"Did you ever see this guy?"

"No. The only time they were together was in Portland. He took her out to dinner there. They flew there once—in a helicopter."

"I guess he really was trying to impress her."

"It wasn't his. It belonged to some friend. Another rich guy."

"When was that?"

"Let's see. It was during dead week of last term. Just before Christmas vacation, I think. I remember she broke a study session with me to go. I didn't know about the helicopter until she got back."

Suddenly, the door burst open and Joel Friedkin stomped in.

"Where the hell . . .? Sorry, Tom. I didn't know you were busy."

"I was about to come over. Joel Friedkin, this is one of my students, April Greer. April, Mr. Friedkin is the director of the advertising spots the university is going to start running on TV soon."

Forever single-minded, Joel barely glanced at April, who had extended her hand.

"Hi, how ya doin'? So, when's this little *tête-à-tête* gonna end? We've still got some shit to do and I need to talk to you."

April stood up and put on her coat. "I'll get out of your way. I'll see you in class Friday, Mr. Martindale."

Joel made no effort move out of earshot and let us conclude our conversation in private. I nudged him aside and followed her out the door into the hall.

"May I keep this?" I held up the card.

"Oh sure. Maybe you can find out who sent it so Mr. Morgan will know who to thank."

And who killed his daughter, I thought.

"I'm going to try. Thanks for coming in. I'll give you extra time with your assignments. Don't worry."

"Thanks, Mr. Martindale. See you later."

She picked up the backpack, heaved it up onto her shoulder, and left.

"You know, Joel, courtesy isn't against the law."

"Yeah, yeah, yeah. I just needed to see you, that's all. We finished the shooting and it went well. Even her air headedness handled her lines without many retakes. I guess my scaring the piss out of her this morning really worked wonders."

"Sounds like it. So more location shooting tomorrow, then back to Portland and the studio?" I asked.

"Right you are, dear buddy. You got that list of footage you ordered and our schedule for tomorrow?"

"It's in my office. I'll get it."

As I turned the knob, I saw that the lock had been drilled. When I opened the door, I couldn't believe my eyes at what I saw.

25

My office had been completely ransacked. The drawers of my desk and filing cabinets were open, their contents strewn around. Whole shelf loads of books had been thrown onto the floor, as if someone had taken his arm, put it behind the books, and pulled.

"Wow, somebody's real mad at you," Joel said as he stuck his head in." A real raging nutcase did this."

As I looked around, I felt personally violated, the same sensation I'd had about twenty years before after my apartment was robbed when I lived in New York.

"He even broke my paperweight."

I reached down and picked up a shell from the coast, now broken into small pieces.

"This has to be that guy from U of O, the one you had the run-in with."

"Why would he be that stupid?"

"How'd he get in?"

"The outer door was unlocked when I got back. Gates was probably waiting for the caterers to leave and saw his chance, and broke this lock."

I motioned for Joel to sit in one of the chairs. At the moment, all of them were overturned. He picked one up and sat down. I did the same with the chair at my desk. Then I picked up the phone, and punched in a number.

"Angela, this is Tom Martindale," I said into Lieutenant Pride's voice mail in my best radio voice. "My office has been vandalized and I think I know who did it. Please call me."

I looked at Joel, who seemed genuinely sorry over what had happened. This was the first time I had ever seen him express any emotion other than haughtiness.

"My friend who heads the Oregon State Police detachment on campus. She helps me out from time to time."

"A good person to know . . . Look, I'm really sorry about all of this, but I need to do some things. Do you suppose that list is somewhere around?"

"List?"

I was drawing a blank.

"Before I opened the door to all of this, you were going to give me a list of the film footage you ordered and the schedule for tomorrow."

"God. Of course, I forgot in all the excitement. It was in here, but now it's gone. He probably took it. It won't tell him much without the script. The list is in my computer. I'll print out another copy for you. He didn't find the disk with the ad stuff on it. I had labeled it 'J Seminar.'"

I turned on my machine and waited for the screen to come to life.

"He wouldn't have been able to get in here without my password. I doubt he had time to fool around and break into it to get the script."

I typed in the magic word and found what I wanted and brought it to the screen. I had put the schedule and the list of film footage into the same memo. I turned on the printer and commanded it to do its stuff.

"I'll have what you want in a minute, Joel."

I took the pages out of the printer and stapled them together.

"Thanks, Tom. You want some help with this mess?"

"No, I think I'd better wait for the police. I don't expect them to treat it like a major crime, but I would like my friend to take a look at it."

Joel stood up.

"See you in the morning then."

"You all set for dinner?"

"Oh sure. I've been thinking I need to take Patsy out—to show her I appreciate what she does for me. I know I treat her like shit half the time!"

"Half the time?" I said with a laugh.

"Message received. What's the best restaurant in town?"

"The Gables, on Ninth Street. It's fairly close to your hotel."

"I'll find it. I'll see you. Don't let this upset you. Just think of it as one of life's little tests."

"Yeah, I guess. See you tomorrow."

He walked to the outer door and was gone. The phone rang as I sat down to print out another copy of the memo.

"Hello."

"Tom. It's Angela. I got your message."

"My office was vandalized and . . ."

"I'll be right over. Just sit tight and try not to touch anything."

After hanging up, I walked back out into the conference room, closing the door to my office. I locked the outer door and turned out the lights. I didn't need any interruptions just now.

I was fairly certain who had ruined my office, but was it linked to my main concern: who had killed Emily Morgan and Duke Ramsay? The same person had probably killed both of them, but who, and why? I had ruled out Del Johnson, so that left another student, a stranger or someone in the athletic department. Even thinking that made me queasy.

Someone tried the door.

"Tom. Are you in there?"

I unlocked the door and opened it.

"Angela. Come in. Thanks for coming."

The tall officer walked in and took off her hat.

"May I?" she motioned toward the closed door to my inner sanctum.

"Sure, go on in. It's a real mess."

"Some real rage here along with signs of a search, I suppose."

I handed her the memo.

"This is what he was looking for—or part of what he was looking for. It deals with that TV ad we're shooting on campus. He got the memo but he didn't get a copy of the script because I had it with me."

The sound of triumph in my voice rang rather hollow as I looked around at the ruined surroundings.

"You keep saying 'he.' Do you know who did this?"

"His name is Charles Gates. He's got a position in the public affairs office at the U of O. He runs their ad program. For some reason, he's become obsessed since he heard we are working on this ad campaign. It's like he's trying to stop us so we won't compete with him. I mean he's very blatant about it. He makes no attempt to hide what he does. Just this morning, he made a scene out on the Quad . . ."

"Oh, he's the one Trooper Bergstrom was telling me about. The guy who created a stir at the MU?"

"That's him. Another thing, Angela. Joel Friedkin, the director, saw him talking to Emily Morgan during our shoot in Portland. It may be nothing, but I thought I should tell you."

"Yeah, I'll look into it. So you think he came in here and did this?"

I nodded.

"How did he get in?"

"The caterers served lunch to the film crew from here. When they cleaned up, they just closed the door. They knew I was coming back. There was maybe a thirty-minute gap between the time they left and I arrived. He must have been watching for his chance."

"Sounds pretty convincing to me. I'll get one of our technicians to see if he can get some identifiable prints. We don't usually do that, but this sounds like it could get political and touchy, I mean the two rival schools and all. We'll need to back up your suspicions with something more concrete. I'll call my counterpart at the U of O and see what he knows about this Gates person."

"Thanks, Angela. I appreciate it. Can you sit down for a minute?"

She motioned to the conference room and we both walked in there.

"Anything new on the Morgan and Ramsay cases?"

"I can't say much since they're on-going investigations."

"I realize that, but I do have more than a casual interest in both cases."

"I know you were friends of both the victims. Off the record, we don't have any strong leads yet. The crime lab in Salem is conducting tests on clothing, et cetera. Results won't be known for a while. The autopsies didn't reveal a hell of a lot, beyond what killed them, which we had pretty much guessed."

"I've got a theory about both cases."

"Here we go again! The investigative reporter turned master detective is swinging into action."

She was smiling, but I knew she would just as soon have me butt out of this. I also felt I had to be careful what I said, lest I reveal anything about Del Johnson that would make Angela more suspicious than she already was.

"Okay. It's your funeral. If you want to wind up in charge of an office in Dufur or Drain or some other godforsaken place, keep ignoring me," I laughed. "You know the campus is quite jittery about this. Worried parents are calling the president's staff and the deans."

"Yeah," she replied. "I'm feeling the heat. The president called me to his office this morning to discuss my investigation. I know I've got to come up with something soon. I thought an assignment to a place like this would be restful. I didn't expect to be in the middle of two murder investigations."

"I believe it's only the second time someone has been killed on campus. The only other time was in 1972, just after I came here. A girl was killed in her dorm room by a male student who went temporarily nuts."

"I was just reading the case file on that yesterday," she added, looking at me in a let's-quit-beating-around-the-bush way. "Go ahead and tell me what you've found out."

"It's not what I found out, it's what I suspect. I don't have any facts, just suspicions."

"Tell me what you're talking about!"

"I mentioned last week about the coach's wife, Gloria Martino, and the players and how that might be connected to Emily Morgan's death."

"Yeah, but you had no proof. Do you now? Has something turned up?"

"Not really, but I have come to the conclusion that the killer is someone who works in the athletic department."

"That's crazy, Tom. Someone associated with our team a killer? Come on, Tom. Come off it! I can't see it."

"I admit it's a stretch. It seems to me, though, that someone down there was trying to silence Emily and Duke to keep them from telling what they knew."

"Yes, but know about what?"

"That I haven't figured out, maybe faking grades or sleeping with Mrs. M."

"I trust your instincts, Tom, but I don't know how to delve into this without causing a real brouhaha. If the state police start nosing around, the shit is going to hit the fan. I've got to have something more to go on. Let's talk about it when I get the lab results back. Maybe something will turn up."

"Right. So when will that technician go over the place?"

"This afternoon."

She got up to leave.

"Stay out of police business, Tom. It's dangerous and you might mess up our work."

I gave her a half-hearted smile, but said nothing.

26

From time to time in the years I have lived in Corvallis, one company or another had tried to establish commercial air service to Portland. With all those faculty people traveling constantly, they reasoned, a small feeder airline couldn't lose. No matter how much financial backing they secured—or how much ballyhoo they generated during the launch—the airlines in question never lasted very long. For reasons known only to them, Corvallis people preferred instead to spend an hour and a half driving to the Portland airport or forty minutes to the smaller terminal in Eugene.

Despite this, however, Corvallis has an airport. In fact, with business from private planes, corporate jets, and freight companies, the airport is thriving.

It was four thirty when I pulled up in front of the main building. Inside, I headed for a section labeled "Charter Service." No one was behind the counter. I waited a few minutes before hitting the brass bell a sign told me to ring for service.

No one appeared so I rang the bell again.

"Hold your horses. Can't a fellow take a leak in peace?"

An enormous man had walked up behind me and was squeezing his body through the entrance to the area behind the counter. He must have weighed

300 pounds. And he didn't seem to be very happy to see a customer. His face was angry, from his permanently furrowed brow to the downward curl of his mouth, surrounded by a Fu Manchu mustache. His nametag read Lyle.

"Sorry. I didn't see anyone around so I did what the sign told me to do."

"I don't see any lips on that sign. What can you do me for?"

His little variation on the standard questions of clerks everywhere seemed to amuse him because he smiled. I waited for his face to start to crack at any time.

"Do you charter helicopters?"

"Do I look like the Air National Guard?"

"I take that as a no."

He glowered.

"Does anyone rent helicopters at this airport?"

"Do I look like twenty questions?"

I stomped away in disgust, put off by his surly manner. No one else was staffing any of the counters so I walked to an office at the end of the waiting room. It was presided over by a blonde with big hair and a mini-skirt. Her phone rang as she saw me and she held up her hand to delay whatever question I had.

"Mid-Valley Air, good afternoon."

She listened intently to the voice on the other end, occasionally cracking her gum.

"If you have your package here by 6 tonight, it will connect to an eastbound flight in Portland."

She kept cracking her gum.

"Twenty-seven fifty for overnight service."

She slammed the phone down and glared at the receiver.

"Some people want service without paying for it. Me, I believe in full service no matter what."

She smiled at me and leaned forward, her breasts touching the top of the desk in such a way that it made them more prominent than they were on their own. Then she leaned back and uncrossed her legs so fast that her skirt rode up her legs an inch or two. She got up and walked to the counter.

"You got a load you want to deliver?" she asked, her face enveloped in that same smile, although it seemed to have turned into a leer.

"No . . ."

I suddenly felt the need to clear my throat.

"No, just information."

"Too bad. So what do you want to know."

"Where can I find information about helicopter rentals?"

"You want to get high, I'll see to it you don't need a helicopter."

"Heights make me dizzy—and I sometimes get nosebleeds."

"That can get real messy in a hurry."

She winked at me and laughed again, this time a little louder than before.

"Look . . ." I glanced at her nametag " . . . Chantal, I think you're very funny, but I'm in kind of a hurry."

"Aren't they all. You don't have to turn into Mr. Uppity Up. I was just havin' a little fun. I'll be serious, I promise. It's just that you're kinda cute and I thought . . . Never mind what I thought."

"The helicopter, Chantal?"

"Sorry. We're freight forwarders and we use conventional prop planes, no choppers. In fact, no one runs a helicopter charter service here."

"I was led to believe that a helicopter was rented to take someone I know to dinner in Portland. I wanted his name."

"For one night? Wow. That's a high roller I'd like to meet. It might be in the operations manager's records. I help out in his office when Lola isn't there. She's his regular secretary. I could look."

"That would be great. I'd appreciate it very much. It's kind of important."

"Okay, sweetie. Come with me and we'll take a peek. No one's around to stop us."

"That's what I'm afraid of."

We both laughed. Chantal was a real riot.

We walked across the empty waiting room to the operations office. She unlocked the door and turned on the light.

"They all left early to go to some kinda dinner for a big shot city official at the country club."

I followed her to the filing cabinets along the rear wall. She walked to one marked, "Flight Records."

"When was the flight you're interested in?"

"Last December, about the middle of the month."

She opened the top drawer and started shuffling through file folders.

"Here's December. Let's try that."

She pulled out a folder.

"Here, you look through it. I just chipped a fingernail on this damned drawer. You like this glitter?" She held her hands out for me to admire.

"Very nice. Must have been expensive."

"Fifty bucks, if you want to know the truth." She shook her head at the memory of that extravagance.

"There's one sheet for every flight. It should list day, time, type of aircraft, fuel consumed, name of pilot, name of owner, list of passengers."

She handed me the folder, which was thicker than I would have imagined.

"Heavy. Lots of flights, I guess."

Chantal had begun to work on her nail.

"Sweetie, you may think this is some kind of hicksville airport, but it's not."

I sat down at the table and opened the folder. I started at the back and read each sheet of paper—all one hundred of them.

She returned to her impromptu manicure, carefully filing the minute chip.

I found what I wanted on a flight leaving on December 16. It had taken off at three and returned at midnight. The craft was owned by Last Wilderness Lumber Company, Junction City, Oregon. Along with a pilot, the helicopter had carried two passengers to Portland that chilly night seven weeks ago: Emily Morgan and Ricardo Martino.

27

TUESDAY

L ast Wilderness Lumber Company sounded suitably environmental but it had the reputation of being quick to clear-cut a forest, then deal with the outcry later. It was owned by Darrel Granger, a university alum mentioned by Duke Ramsay as a big contributor to both the university foundation and the athletic department.

I found this out after I made a few phone calls and conducted a computer search of several databases. If Granger was a million dollar donor to athletics, he was possibly a close friend of Coach Martino. He was probably always happy to do personal favors for the coach, like take him and a potential sexual conquest to Portland for dinner.

Poor Emily couldn't have realized what was happening. On the rebound from Del, flattered by the attention of an older man, she had gone for a fun evening. Only maybe it hadn't been so much fun. She had spurned Martino's advances and made him angry. But had she made him angry enough for him to kill her? Getting a little sexual action on the side was one thing. Killing a girl who dared to resist was quite another. And seven weeks later isn't exactly spur of the moment rage either.

This was all supposition, of course. I turned off my computer to ponder one other puzzle. What was the Grizzly reference? I thumbed through some notes about Martino I'd made the other day and found my answer. Martino had been the coach at the University of Montana before coming here. The Montana mascot was the grizzly bear.

I reached for the phone and called Del's friend Gabriel Washington at his apartment. I got his machine. As many students do, he had made a real production out of his message. It started with loud music, then switched to his voice rapping out a greeting.

"This is Tom Martindale. I need to see our friend soon."

III

Filming went off without a hitch. Everyone knew their lines and even the weather cooperated for a second day. Joel was ready to wrap things up after eleven thirty.

"I can't believe how well it's gone today," I said to him as we stood together on lower campus, an area to the east of 14th Street where tall elm trees lined a long, curving path which led to an ornamental gate, gift of the Class of 1907. It has always been one of my favorite parts of campus.

"Once in a while, things fool you that way," Joel answered. "They fool you by going according to the goddamn plan. I can't believe it either."

He then moved to the side of the camera. Filming was beginning again. Sara and Sam were strolling toward us, talking about how much their futures depended on this university.

"Cut. That's a wrap. Pack things up kids. We're out of here. Patsy."

His dutiful assistant came running over to carry out his order. While he pondered the big picture, she would make sure everything got packed up and everybody fed. I had seen the caterers park on the street at the end of the path and I suddenly got hungry.

At that moment Sara and Sam rushed up to me.

"Wow! That was really cool! Thanks for letting me be a part of this."

I shook Sam's outstretched hand. "Thank you for all your hard work."

Sara gave me a big kiss on the cheek.

"Everything you've done for us has been totally awesome!"

"Both of you have done a good job. I appreciate what you've done. The university appreciates what you did. I think you'll be proud of the work too. I'll make sure you get copies."

Patsy hustled over to us.

"Come on, you kids. I'll get you out of that makeup."

The three of them turned and walked toward the motor home. I headed for the catering truck. The two "Rose City Baguettes"—as the stitching on their matching outfits read—were setting up food on two large folding tables under the trees. In the middle of a park far from electrical outlets and water faucets, they had somehow managed to fix chicken fajitas, nachos, refried beans, and a huge taco salad.

I was the first in line to eat. I filled my china plate and went over to sit under a tree. I was halfway through my meal when I noticed a bright yellow Corvette driving slowly down the adjoining street. Because the top was down, I could see the driver very clearly. Kurt Blake saw me recognize him and tipped his cap. Then he drove off in a screech of tires.

I I I

Jack Jennings was waiting outside my office when I arrived there a bit after 1:30.

"Professor Martindale, I need to talk to you."

"Sure, Jack. Come in."

I unlocked the door and started toward the closed door of the inner office. Then I remembered the mess.

"Let's just sit out here."

"I did some checking down at the athletic department, just superficial stuff. As you taught us, you can get a lot by playing dumb and talking to secretaries who really know what's going on."

"I've created a monster here," I laughed. "So what did my tried-and-true system unearth?"

"I made some calls to my football friends and came up with a list of four black players that were dropped from the team when their eligibility was up and they didn't get degrees. Three of them are working in fast food joints, the fourth is at a community college in Portland, really struggling to get a degree. I've made contact with two of them and I'm going up to Portland this weekend to interview them. I think they're bitter enough that they'll talk freely. After I've seen them, then I'll go to the coach and athletic director and get their side. I need the stuff from the players first."

"Good approach. Get all your ducks in a row, so to speak."

"Or beavers."

We both laughed.

"Oh yeah, one other thing. This other matter—the sex stuff. I talked to my girlfriend. She didn't know anything about it. I mean she said they hadn't heard any rumors. But she was going to talk to her old roommate who is still a rally squad member."

"Did she give you a name?"

I asked the question casually, hoping I wouldn't get one particular answer.

He looked through his notes.

"Tiffanie something."

One of the women with Kurt Blake at the shoot yesterday. Worse, she was one of the women with the coach on Cape Foulweather.

"Jack, I think your investigation may have encountered a little snag."

28

"What do you mean? What's so special about Tiffanie what's-her-name?"

"Don't tell your girlfriend, but I think she's one of the coach's special friends."

"I see what you mean! So now you think the coach knows that I've been looking into things?"

I nodded, smiling weakly.

"But what's he going to do? He can sue me for libel if I do a story and get the facts wrong, but I won't get them wrong. He can freeze out our sports reporters. We can live with that. I'm not worried. I can handle any of that."

"I wouldn't get too cocky, Jack. But I'm concerned about something else. Did you ever hear of Kurt Blake?"

He shook his head.

"He claims to be Mrs. Martino's nephew. He's also a business partner in a bed and breakfast the coach and his wife bought into up on Cape Foulweather on the coast. But I've seen him with Tiffanie and another girl, Shannon. I'm sure Tiffanie ran right to him to tell him you were asking questions. The guy is ruthless from what I've seen. I think you'd better pull back on your reporting until we figure this out."

"Look, Mr. Martindale, I was a logger. I don't scare easily. I can take care of myself."

"That may be true, but be prepared. Blake'll come at you when you aren't expecting it."

"But why? What's he got to hide?"

"Two murders, for one thing. I wouldn't be at all surprised to find out that he was involved in both the Emily Morgan and Duke Ramsay killings. I haven't sorted it all out yet, but all paths seem to be leading to the Blake character and the Martinos. I don't know if it's sex or eligibility shortcuts for players or both. It still doesn't make sense to me."

We parted soon after, with Jack agreeing to let me know what he found out in his interviews with the athletes. I didn't promise him as much, largely because I didn't think I should tell him all I knew about Del and Emily. I could get into that later, if necessary.

| | |

WEDNESDAY

The next day I went back to my classes but I was preoccupied with all the events of the past week. It was hard to concentrate on something as mundane as the different kinds of feature stories that exist in journalism when so much else was going on in my life.

After class, I was walking back to my office when Gabriel Washington suddenly appeared at my side. He used the same "returning your book" subterfuge he had used before. I played along.

"Thanks, Gabe. I'm glad you enjoyed the book."

He smiled, handed me the book, and peeled off down the stairs. I didn't think anyone was actually watching us, but, these days, who could say for sure? I tucked the book under my arm until I was inside my office. As before, a note was tucked into its pages:

"Peavy Arboretum, 3 p.m.

I tore it into tiny pieces and put them in my pocket. I locked my outer door and went into my office. Pride had left a message that the technician had finished his work. It was time to straighten up my office. I was finished in about an hour.

I bought my lunch and ate it in the student union lounge, while listening to a Mozart sonata performed as part of the annual Winter Music Festival. It was nice to lose myself in something other than murder.

I got back to my office at about 1:30 and decided to check my e-mail. I turned on my computer to find that I had nine messages. I ignored all but the one from Hadley Collins:

Hi, Tom. Before I left town for a trip to Washington, D.C., I wanted to let you know that our friend Gates has been quietly fired from the U of O. I told my counterpart there what we think happened and we agreed that everyone concerned would be better off if he would go quietly. Surprisingly, Gates agreed. We won't press charges for the suspected break-in if he just goes away. I assume that is satisfactory with you? I talked Lt. Pride of the Oregon State Police and she said she hadn't found any link between Gates and Emily. Their chat was just that, I guess. By the way, you will be interested in knowing that he was once institutionalized for mental illness. I guess that information didn't turn up at the time he was hired. Good luck on the rest of your "shoot." I'll look forward to a progress report when I get back. Hadley

Sure, I thought, things will be great if he really does go away. I just hoped that what happened to him—and my part in it—wouldn't send him around the bend again. As much as I would have liked to punish Gates, I suppose a hushed-up resignation was for the best. I replied to Hadley's message by saying just that.

When I turned off my computer I noticed the red light on my phone blinking. I dialed the proper code and got a knot in my stomach from the message. It was from Jack Jennings, his voice no longer filled with logger bravado.

"Professor Martindale. I need to see you at Cape Foulweather tonight. I'm in some trouble."

I hung up, knowing without a doubt that Blake had him and was using that fact to get me over to the coast, too. I had no choice but to go there. I was no mindless hero, but I had gotten Jack into this in the first place. I felt sick as I dialed Pride's number.

I got her recorded message and followed directions to speak to a real person: the receptionist in the public safety office.

"Is Angela Pride around?"

"May I ask what is the nature of your call?"

She sounded like she was reading from a prepared text.

"It's personal. Is she there?"

My voice was getting an edge to it.

"She is attending a commander's meeting in Salem."

"When will she be back?"

"She thought the meeting would last until four. She'll probably come back in the office about before heading home."

"Thanks for the information."

I dialed her number again and left a detailed message about what had happened.

| | |

Twenty minutes later, I pulled into the parking lot of the Peavy Arboretum Lodge, a rustic building set on the edge of the university's experimental forest. Its thousands of trees, spread over several hundred acres north of town, were managed by faculty and researchers in the College of Forestry. The lodge serves as a pleasant meeting place away from campus but not so far that it takes long to get here.

Luckily, nothing had been booked for today. The building was dark as I got out of my car and stood so Del could see me. Then I walked down the hill to the pond and then across a field and onto the logging road into the forest, long a popular destination for hikers and bicyclists. Private cars were not permitted beyond the chain that blocked the way at the edge of the pavement.

Two joggers ran past me as I headed up the road. After about a half mile, I sat down on a felled log near a large boulder.

"Don't turn around or act like you've heard me. Walk back into the woods to your right."

I sat nonchalantly for a minute or so as if I was enjoying the surroundings. Then I got up and followed Del's directions. The trees were close together here and the forest suddenly got very thick. It would be easy for us to keep out of sight here.

"Hello, Mr. Martindale. I'm glad to see you."

Del was standing by a tall Douglas fir, dressed in dark clothing. I could barely distinguish him from the trees.

29

"It's good to see you too, Del, but we don't have time for small talk. You need to go with me to the coast, right now!"

He looked at me like I was crazy.

"No way, man. I'm keepin' out of sight!"

"I'm this close to figuring out what happened."

I held up my thumb and forefinger, a scant half inch from one another.

"You mean to Emily? And Duke Ramsay?"

"That's exactly what I mean. I think the killer is waiting for us at Martino's place at Cape Foulweather. I'll explain everything on the way."

"But what about the cops?"

"You're going to have to trust me like you've never trusted anyone else before. Are you willing to do that?"

He hesitated for a moment, then nodded his agreement.

"You got a car?"

"No, Gabe picked me up in Portland and drove me here. Then he split."

"My car's parked near the lodge. Work your way back around to the parking lot. Stay in the trees until I drive to the edge of the lot."

We parted and I hiked quickly down the trail to my car. As we arranged, I drove it to the side nearest the trees. I had put down the rear seat making an area where Del could lie down and be hidden and still breath. That way, we could get out of town without anybody seeing him. I popped the trunk release and waited.

Del ran to the car and got in, folding his tall frame into the small space and covering himself with a blanket.

"Are you all right back there?"

"Kinda close quarters, but I'll live."

"As soon as it gets dark, you can come up front.

I pulled slowly out of the parking lot, then down the road to the main gate of the arboretum. I drove south on the side road, eventually driving in the same direction on Highway 99W. I took the Walnut Boulevard bypass around Corvallis.

We were cruising easily through Philomath, a small town to the west, when I saw the unmistakable flashing lights of a police car in my rearview mirror.

"Shit."

"Good afternoon, officer."

A rather fat city policeman was peering in at me as I rolled down the window. The uniform he was wearing had either been issued to someone else or he needed to go on a crash diet.

"Good afternoon, sir. May I see your license and registration?"

"Certainly."

I pulled my license out of my wallet. I opened the glove compartment and quickly found the car registration in the plastic case I kept it in.

"Here you are. Could you tell me . . ."

He put up his hand to halt my question.

"In good time, sir. In good time."

He carried both documents back to his patrol car and sat behind the wheel. I could see him talking on his radio.

"Don't panic, Del," I whispered through clenched teeth. "It's just routine. Stay calm."

In the rearview mirror I could see that he had finished his call and was getting back out. He was back at my window in seconds.

"Here you are, sir," the policeman said as he handed me my license and registration.

"Thank you."

"I stopped you because you didn't have your lights on. You know, on these dark winter days, it's a good idea to turn on your lights, even in the daytime."

I smiled and nodded, listening intently to Lecture #25 from the Police Academy.

"You're going over the Coast Range?"

"Yes, I am."

"Well that's even more reason to turn them on. Why not do it now and I'll check them?"

"Here goes."

I turned the proper knob as he waddled to the front. He looked from one headlight to the other, then back again.

"My God, what an idiot." I whispered to myself as he walked back towards me.

"Good. They look good."

He smiled and glanced at the rear interior of the car. Had Del moved? Had he heard something that would cause him to ask me to open the trunk?

"You haulin' something back there?"

"Yes, I've been moving some . . . books this morning, yeah books."

"The trunk's not big enough to hold those boxes?

"No, I pull the rear seat forward and it makes it like a station wagon back there. Want to see?"

I held my breath as I reached around like I was going to disengage the trunk latch. Even though I imagined Del was well hidden under the blankets, I hoped I wouldn't have to test my supposition.

"That's real neat, mister. These older models had a lot of good features, didn't they? Nice for an older man to have a sports car like this. You restore it yourself?"

"I'm not very good at that," I smiled agreeably. "I was lucky to find it." I wanted to get out of here but dared not make the first move.

"Thanks for showin' me. Now you have a real nice day, sir, and drive carefully."

"I will, officer. Thanks."

He stepped out of the way as I started the engine and pulled out onto the highway, carefully using my left turn signal to indicate the direction as I did so. In the rearview mirror I could see him making a U-turn to head back into town, no doubt getting ready for another "lights on for safety" lecture.

I turned onto a logging road and stopped so Del could get out.

"Man, am I glad to be out of that coffin, I'll tell you that! I felt like I was dead and buried!"

"Sorry about that. I didn't know how else to smuggle you out of town. Here, have some juice."

I passed him the thermos.

"How about an apple?"

I tossed him one.

"It'll put some moisture back in your mouth."

"Man, you've thought of everything!"

"I wasn't sure if you'd come along but I prepared just in case. There's a candy bar in this bag too."

Although it was nearly dark, we could still see the dim silhouettes of the trees in the forest. We sat on a log and I took a deep breath to inhale the cold crisp air. The aroma of the tree sap and needles was wonderful.

"Does this get to you like it does me—I mean the majesty of this place— the smell, the quiet? It's like a cathedral."

"It's great, but I'm a big city kid. I need to smell a little smog in the air, too."

We both laughed and sat for a time enjoying the quiet.

After a while, I broke the silence. "I hate to disturb our rest period, but we've got to get moving."

We got into my car and I backed around, headed out of the logging road and turned west on Highway 20. I plunged right into what I had to say, hoping it would give him a reason to think that his nightmare would soon be over.

"Let me lay it out for you. I think both the coach and his wife were somehow involved in Emily's murder. The coach was after Emily . . ."

"You mean in a sexual way?"

"That's exactly what I mean."

"That bastard. Did he get Em pregnant?"

"He is not at the top of my list."

"I know. It looks bad for me, but I swear I didn't know. She didn't tell me."

"Even that last night?"

"No, not even then." Tears were running down his face by this time and he looked away.

"Did Mrs. M know about the coach making a play for Emily?"

"It's only a guess, but I doubt that she cared, as long as he let her do her own playing around."

"You mean like when she came on to me?"

"Exactly. Do you know about other players she propositioned?"

"I'm not sure."

"Come on, Del! Quit protecting her because she's your coach's wife."

"It's just that she . . . both of them, she and Coach Martino, always treated me well."

He thought for a minute. "Yeah. I see what you mean. I guess I was naive."

"That's putting it mildly. What about the other players?"

"You know about Bobby Hardy."

"Yeah, I know a lot about that."

"There were a couple of university administrators she said she had one-night stands with. I remember one guy from the alumni office she said wouldn't take no for an answer. But mostly she liked younger guys."

"Like football players."

"Yeah, like football players. Besides Hardy, there was Gabe."

"Your old friend?"

He sighed and nodded.

"I can't believe it! I mean he's a nice kid but he's not big in the brain department and he's slightly paunchy."

"He's a lineman, Professor Martindale. They have to be big. Maybe that's what attracted her, plus maybe the adventure of going to bed with a black man. I don't know."

"Did this happen after you turned her down?"

"I guess. He didn't tell me about it for a long time. I think he was ashamed about it."

"Did she make any moves on you besides that one time?"

"Not really. She just flirted a lot and we kind of sparred around verbally. I tried to tell Gabe that she was using him and playing him for a fool but I think he really thought she cared for him. He got so he'd get real mad when I brought it up so I just quit saying anything."

"When were they together for the last time?"

"Around Christmas, I think. I went home to California but Gabe stayed here. They got together somewhere. I talked to him about it, I mean I tried to make him see how fruitless the situation was. Emily talked to him too."

"Emily knew about this?"

"Yeah, I told her because I knew she cared about Gabe. By that time, she'd been tutoring him for about a year."

"Did she talk to Gabe?"

"She tried, but he told her it wasn't any of her business, so she quit trying."

"Now let's talk about the coach. Have you ever heard of Last Wilderness Lumber Company and a man named Darrel Granger?"

"Sure. He's a friend of Coach Martino and a big contributor to the athletic department. He comes to social events for the team. I don't know him well, but he's always been nice to me and the other guys."

"Did you know he has a helicopter?"

"Hadn't heard that."

"Well, he loaned it to the coach so he could take Emily to Portland for dinner."

"So that's when the coach was hitting on Em? How do you know that?"

"Get my briefcase from behind the seat."

He pulled it out.

"On top there should be a copy of a flight report that lists the passengers on a flight to Portland last month by the Last Wilderness helicopter."

He read for a minute. "That low-life bastard."

"I don't think Emily did anything wrong. I think she turned him down. She never mentioned it?"

"No, never. Of course we had broken up by then."

"When did you . . ."

"Have sex for the last time?"

I nodded.

"Just before I left town for Christmas. We said we'd do it for old time's sake. I can't see why Emily would go with Martino."

"Her roommate said she was intrigued that someone would fly her out of town for dinner."

"So what does this all mean?"

We had long since reached Newport and turned north on Highway 101. We would arrive at our destination in about fifteen minutes.

"A couple of days ago, I very stupidly brought Jack Jennings, the editor of the student newspaper, into all of this. I have been keeping away from the police to avoid answering questions about you. So I thought Jack could dig into this and stir things up. He's a tenacious reporter and I knew he wouldn't give up until he uncovered all the dirt in the athletic department. Unfortunately, Kurt Blake must have figured out what he was doing. Jack called me this afternoon sounding scared. I think Blake and the Martinos are holding him at their place on Cape Foulweather, I guess to lure me over here. I got him into this, so I have to try to help him."

"Wow. This is really heavy."

"I've left a message for my state police friend. I know she'll help us if she gets here in time. But I can't wait. I don't think they'd hurt Jack, but they may have killed two people already."

I had just finished telling him my plan as we pulled into the Cape Foulweather visitor's parking lot. Fortunately, it was empty. I once again backed my car into the most remote space so it was facing the highway. I figured we would need to make an even faster departure than before and I wanted to be ready.

30

As I had done the week before, we eased along the fence on the north side of the property, headed for the edge where we could slip around the post. This time, I had brought along a penlight for each of us to guide our way when necessary.

"It's not too far along this trail," I whispered. "We'll be at the edge in a minute or so."

We moved along swiftly. My adrenaline was pumping so much that I wasn't even out of breath. I did have trouble keeping up with Del, however. A good athlete, he was in much better shape.

"Real pretty up here," he said. "I wish I could see it in the daytime."

We reached the edge of the cliff and stopped.

He turned his head toward the ocean, which we could hear but not see.

"Before long, I won't be seeing much of anything but four walls," he said sadly.

"Look, if everything goes like I plan tonight, you won't have anything more to worry about."

I hoped I was right.

I stepped over the edge and grabbed the corner post of the chain-link fence. As I held on, I swung one foot around and planted it firmly on the ground inside the fence. I tried to ignore the deafening sound of the surf crashing onto the rocks several hundred feet below me. I definitely did not look down as I made a slight leap to bring my other foot around. Even though it was dark, I thought a glance anywhere but up might cause me to lose my balance at the mere thought of falling.

"There. I'm in." I stepped a few paces out of the way to give Del room to maneuver but still be close enough to help him if necessary.

"This is bad, man. I feel like. . . I'm afraid I'll fall."

"No, no, you won't if you don't look down or think about anything but getting around this barrier."

He stepped back and shook his head.

"I'm going to take my chances by going up and over the fence. I feel better about that."

Del, it's eight feet tall! You can't climb over that!"

"I'm used to going over walls with no foot holds in our practice sessions. This'll be easier that that."

"Okay. You know best. But we need to get out of here. It makes me nervous to stay in one spot."

Del walked back along the fence, picked his spot and had clambered up the fence and dropped to the ground in a rolling landing in seconds.

I was prepared for the Martino's dog this time. My pockets were full of bits of liver wrapped in plastic bags. I had read that liver would preoccupy even the most vicious mastiff. We would soon find out.

We crept along the path to the back of the house, reaching the pool in several minutes. Although the pool area was dark, lights were blazing at the end of the building and we headed in that direction. I remembered the large picture window where I had seen Martino cavorting with the two cheerleaders the week before.

And there he was. Jack Jennings was tied to a chair in front of the window. He was talking to someone out of my view and he didn't look at all happy.

"That's him," I whispered. "They've got him staked out where I couldn't miss him. I'm going to go around to the other side. You stay out of sight until we see what happens. If you hear anything on the road, go up to the gate and tell Lieutenant Pride what I'm doing. She'll figure out how to get in the gate."

Del nodded and stepped farther back in the forest. I made my way across through the trees that bordered the front of the property. Several cars were parked in front of the inn, including Blake's Corvette. Just as I stepped onto the driveway, the front door opened and Kiva came running out the door and headed right for me. He caught up to me in seconds, ignoring my offers of liver.

"Funny thing about Kiva. He's never liked liver."

Kurt Blake stepped out of the woods to my right, carrying a rifle.

"Kiva, stay," he said with a smile as he motioned for me to walk ahead of him toward the house.

"Move!"

We stepped into a two-story room that was the lobby of the inn. A registration desk was straight ahead flanked by twin curving staircases leading to the second floor.

"Go in there."

He nudged me forward, using his rifle.

We entered a large room with a stone fireplace and a number of sofas, chairs, and tables.

There was Jack.

"I never thought I'd be so glad to see one of my professors," he said, a relieved look on his face.

"This is a hell of a way to get out of that term paper."

"Cut the comedy act, Martindale. Join your friend on that other chair."

"You seem all right, Jack."

"I'm just tired."

"Kurt. Is that you?"

Gloria Martino walked in behind Blake, carrying a tray of sandwiches.

"I was getting our guest some fo . . ."

She stopped in her tracks when she saw me. I waited for a sign of recognition, not really sure how that would affect this situation.

"Well, who is this handsome gentleman?"

She gave me a big smile and crossed to a table in front of Jack and me. I smiled back in spite of my growing anxiety. We were in hot water up to our necks.

"Cut the show, Gloria. This is that professor who's been nosing around."

"Oh Kurt. You're no fun anymore. You're always worrying."

I broke into their squabbling in my most chivalrous tone. I stood up and extended my hand to Gloria Martino.

"Mrs. Martino, I'm Tom Martindale. I've seen you around campus."

She smiled again and we shook hands, her face rather blank. God! How could she not remember me! It had only been a few days since we met in the parking lot. So much for my devastating effect on women!

"Jesus Christ, Gloria! This isn't some kind of faculty tea. Get away from him! I've got to think!"

Blake ran his hand up his face and back over his shaved head.

"About what, Blake? About how you killed Emily Morgan?" I asked.

"Who?" Blake seemed genuinely perplexed. "I don't know what you're talking about."

I continued with my direct approach, deciding, perhaps foolhardily, that he wouldn't kill me in front of witnesses. Also, I wanted the tape recorder in my pocket to record everything in case I didn't make it out of here alive.

"And what about Duke Ramsay? Why'd you need to get rid of him?"

"Shut up! Just shut up about that!" he shouted, waving the rifle at me.

"Did he know too much about your role as a procurer for Coach Martino and his wife?"

He stepped forward and hit me hard across the face with his hand.

"Shut the fuck up or I'll use this gun next time and not my hand."

My face started burning and I rubbed it. At least it wasn't bleeding.

"Kurt, darling. You're getting much too upset over nothing."

Gloria went over to Blake and started massaging his shoulders. He relaxed a bit and even smiled at her. She seemed to be trying to defuse the situation.

"Mrs. Martino, maybe you can help make this right. If you let us go now, we won't press charges."

She stepped away from him and walked over to me.

"Honey, I quit believing in tall tales like that when I quit believing in the tooth fairy."

"All right, then. If you're going to kill us, fine. Just tell me how you did it, how you killed Emily Morgan and Duke Ramsay," I said, hoping my tape recorder was getting all this.

Blake seemed to regain his composure and his cockiness.

"Yeah, Sherlock. I'll tell you everything. Pretty soon you'll be going to that lecture hall in the sky and it won't matter anyway. I don't know anything about how the Morgan chick got killed. Ramsay got to nosing around and asking questions about cheating and grades and eligibility. After I found out who you were, I told Gloria he was having lunch with you and she got worried." He turned to look at Gloria, who seemed not to be appreciating his sudden candor.

"You didn't want your little apple cart upset by Ricky losing his job, did you?" He turned back to me.

"Gloria lured Ramsay out to the bridge. I borrowed Bobby Hardy's cycle for her and we rode out to that bridge together and took care of him."

Despite the gravity of the situation, I had to squelch a smile at the thought of Gloria Martino wearing a leather ensemble and straddling a Harley. She was not amused by Blake's revelation.

"Now just a minute, Buster Brown! I told you just to scare him, not to kill him!"

Gloria Martino stepped away from her nephew, a startled look on her face. She thought for a moment, then resumed her sarcastic tone.

"Can I help it if most of your smarts are below your waist?"

Now it was her turn to get smacked by Blake. This time, however, he didn't use his hand, he used the butt of his rifle. The blow sent her reeling, blood spurting from her lip.

A giant figure burst through the door to the terrace, catching all of us by surprise. Gabriel Washington tackled Kurt Blake and sent his gun skittering across the polished wood floor. The large man began to batter Blake with his fists. Then he grabbed his throat and squeezed.

"You hurt Mrs. Martino. You leave her alone."

We were all shouting at him to stop but he continued to hit the smaller man. Just then, a new voice added to the din.

"Gabe. It's okay. You got him!"

Del Johnson stepped through the ruined door. The big man stopped hitting Blake, whose lifeless body collapsed to the floor. Johnson walked over to his friend and led him to a couch where he sat, head down.

"Are you guys okay?"

"We're fine, Del. We're going to be all right."

"What about me? Doesn't anyone care about me?"

All eyes turned toward Gloria Martino who frantically snatched a small revolver out of her purse. She held it out in front of her. The blood from her altercation with Blake had caked on her mouth.

"Gloria, put . . ."

She whirled around and faced Johnson, a wild look in her eyes.

"Shut up, Del. You bastard. You broke my heart. Out of all these guys, you're the only one I really wanted and you turned me down."

Gloria Martino was crying and waving the gun around wildly.

"Gloria. I didn't mean . . ."

"I told you to shut up."

She pulled the trigger and Del went down, holding his shoulder and writhing in pain. I started to stand.

"Stay where you are, professor, if you want your nice educated head to stay on those nice wide shoulders of yours. You and I and Gabe are going to take a little hike."

She turned to the hapless Gabe who seemed oblivious to everything but his own misery.

"Gabe, Kurt's out cold but tie him up anyway. He won't be going with us."

She motioned to the end table next to me.

"There's rope in that drawer. See those handcuffs there too? We'll put them on the teach here."

"Mrs. M, I don't know . . ."

"Gabe. Listen to me. Do you want to be together like we planned? Do you want to take care of me like you said you would—in Mexico?"

He nodded dully and followed her directions.

"Gabe," I said. "Del's hurt. He may be dying."

"Gabe, don't listen to him," Gloria shouted. "If you want us to be together, put these handcuffs on him, in front so we can drag him along."

Gabe hesitated, but soon followed her directions, but as he stepped in front of me to do so, I felt him slip the key into the pocket of my shirt.

"I'll go with you, but I want the answer to a question first," I said. "Why did you kill Emily Morgan?"

I was looking at her but Gabe answered the question.

"Mrs. M didn't do it. I did," Gabe said softly.

Gloria Martino seemed genuinely astonished. She shook her head at the news. "You silly son of a bitch. You killed for me?" Then, she started laughing, her low chuckle quickly turning into a high-pitched cackle.

"Is that why you did it, Gabe?" I asked.

"It wasn't like that at all. I went to see if she'd be my tutor again. I didn't want to be dropped from the team. I didn't want to be declared ineligible. Besides, I always liked her and I thought maybe if I showed how much, she'd help me with school again. I don't know why, but I tried to kiss her."

"She resisted?" I asked.

"Yeah, she suddenly pulled away, and I lunged for her and she fell against that dumpster in the alley and hit her head. That's where I put her body later. We'd gone out there to talk so we'd have some privacy. I wasn't thinking about Del or Mrs. M. I was thinking about my grades."

"Something I wonder about, if we're kind of baring our souls here: where was your husband when you were seeing so much of his players?" I asked.

She threw her head back and laughed lustily.

"Did he know about your plan to have Ramsay killed?"

She shook her head.

"No, the dumb son of a bitch might have tried to stop us."

Behind her on the floor, Del moaned weakly. Gabe turned toward him with a concerned look on his face. Gloria quickly headed off any change of heart on his part.

"Let's get out of here," she said.

She motioned for us to walk through the door, giving Gabe a big kiss as he passed her. Chump that he was, his return kiss was rather passionate until she pushed him away.

"Come on, honey. We'll have time for that kind of stuff later."

At that moment, police car lights flashed across the frosted panels of the front door windows. Angela Pride was finally riding to my rescue.

"Slight change of plans," Gloria said, forcing us through a door behind the main desk, down a short hall and into the kitchen. We ran along past tiled counter tops and a stove, amid gleaming pots hanging from the recessed ceiling.

"Out that door," she shouted, pointing with the gun.

We were now on the deck surrounding the pool and she spurred us on around it toward the forest beyond.

"Kiva. Come," Gloria said as we headed for the forest.

In a second or two, her galloping Doberman seemed to be enjoying this game his mistress was playing. Our strange entourage reached the edge of the cliff in a few minutes.

"Gabe. Back away from him," she said.

The big man did as he was told, but then she raised her gun and calmly shot him in the chest. A startled look remained on his face as he fell to the ground.

"You may be kinda cute, but you've got a smart mouth," she said to me. "I think you'd be arguing with me all the time about everything. I like my men compliant."

Her ego had once again prevailed and she had us on the lam together, hurling witty bon mots back and forth as we lazed away the days in bed in posh hotels overseas.

Before she could shoot me, I lunged for the gun. As the big dog saw me attack his mistress, he leaped in the air, aiming for my throat. By this time I had engaged Gloria's hand. Although I dodged enough to deter the dog from connecting with my throat, his fangs sank into my hand.

The combined forces sent all of us over the cliff. As I fell, Gloria's screams were drowned out by the sound of the waves crashing on the jagged rocks below.

III

Falling through the air gives you an odd feeling—I mean beyond the mind-numbing fear. It has a strange sense of weightlessness about it.

The dog released his grip on my hand as soon as we started to tumble. He now had other concerns on his mind than coming to the aid of his mistress. I parted company with my flight companions when my feet left the edge of the cliff. I didn't see either Gloria or the dog again.

Just then I landed on a small ledge. I couldn't believe my good luck, but it was short-lived. My body seemed determined to continue downward. Just as I braced for my plunge to certain death, my flailing hands caught hold of a twisted tree growing out of the surface of the ledge. My handcuffs caught its sturdy branches and I held on tight with both hands.

At first my legs were kicking the air. Then, one foot came to rest in an indentation on the cliff. I tested its strength and my foot held. I was then able to use it as a toehold and pull myself up onto the ledge. I caught my breath and took stock of the situation. If the handcuffs held, I would be all right. But what if they didn't? Even if I survived the fall into the sea below, I would die from hypothermia once I hit the water. Before that, the waves would batter me against the rocks. Indeed, the din of that crashing drowned out all other sounds now. I couldn't really think for all the noise. The wind had come up and it began to rain, adding to my misery and sense of hopelessness.

". . . anybody . . . there?"

The wind and rain were really playing tricks on my ears. I thought I heard a voice, but it seemed thunderous and omnipresent. I was probably hallucinating.

"Martin . . . send someone . . . police."

At that, I stood up and looked up the cliff side to the top where I could see the flickering beams of flashlights above

"Down here!"

My words seemed to be carried away with the wind. I've never been a good shouter

At about that point, the wind suddenly subsided and the rain ceased. It was actually quiet.

"Tom, it that you?"

It was Angela Pride.

I felt hope but then rocks started falling on me and I lost consciousness.

32

THURSDAY

I knew I was in a hospital when I was awakened by the smell, a combination of cleaning solvents and medicine and bodily odors that usually makes me want to gag even when I'm just visiting someone.

The room was fuzzy at first, then I could make out two figures standing at the foot of my bed.

"You two friends now?" I asked, focusing on Angela Pride and Del Johnson.

I moved my hands together to indicate their sudden friendship. My lips were so thick it was hard to talk.

"Water?"

Angela handed me a glass with one of those crooked straws. I drank several swallows and motioned for her to take it away.

"Glad you're back with us. You passed out."

"How long?"

"Since last night."

"Where am I?"

"Good Samaritan in Corvallis. The Coast Guard brought you here after one of their guys rescued you."

"How did they get into the act?"

"I called them when we figured out you were down there. I figured that they had more experience than we did in plucking people off ledges along the coast. They got there fairly fast, but when one of their guys started down the cliff, he loosened some rocks so he came back up."

"And one of the rocks hit me on the head and knocked me out?"

"When he got to you, you were curled up like a baby, unconscious. He brought you up on a harness."

"Amazing! But what happened to everybody else? I know about Gloria Martino and her dog. He leaped to save her from me and that's what sent us flying."

"Gabe and Kurt Blake are both dead," Del said, stepping forward and speaking for the first time. His right arm was in a sling.

"You all right? You were shot. I remember now."

"Only a flesh wound. My arm will be fine."

"But how did you guys . . ."

I moved my arms toward each other again.

". . . get together, hunter and prey no more?"

"Jack Jennings witnessed everything and verified Del's story," Angela said. "Gabe killed Emily by accident. It wasn't really related to anything more than his own misguided way of getting her to be his tutor again."

"The stupid jerk," added Del, his voice rising in disgust. "God! I thought I knew him."

"Gloria was not involved in Emily's death in any way," continued Angela. "She may have been infatuated with our young friend here, but it didn't drive her to kill a rival as you may have thought. She did get Blake to kill Duke Ramsay because she was afraid he knew too much. Blake's not her nephew, by the way."

"What a surprise," I said.

We all laughed.

"He had a juvenile record and I guess Mrs. Martino's father adopted him years ago. She called him her nephew but he was really her adopted brother.

Very confusing. He and Gloria were lovers on and off over the years."

"Along with half the football team," I said. "So why did the coach tolerate all of these shenanigans?

"He had his own indiscretions to cover up," she answered. "Cheerleaders."

"So is the university making a move against him? He shouldn't be allowed anywhere near college kids, male or female," I said.

"The coach has resigned. Everybody is embarrassed so I guess a lot of what happened will be hushed up for now," Angela said. "The State Police will conduct a thorough investigation."

Del stepped forward and grabbed my hand. "Thanks for believing in me when nobody else did," he said with a sigh.

"That's okay. I did what I did for Emily too. She was a wonderful young woman. It's horrible when such a young person dies so prematurely, so much potential unrealized. I just had to figure all of this out for her too.

Now it was my turn to get all teary.

"And poor Duke Ramsay. I guess I set him up to die—but I just blundered into it."

"You had no way of knowing he'd be killed, Tom," Angela said. "Murder is seldom rational or predictable."

"I'll see you soon, Professor Martindale," said Del as he headed out the door. I waved as Angela stepped closer to the bed.

"I'll get out of here and let you get some rest. I wondered if you and I . . ."

"As my students always say," I laughed. "Awesome!"

| | |

THREE DAYS LATER

I arrived at the meeting of the University Image Enhancement Committee late, on purpose. Given what had happened to me, I felt I deserved a grand entrance. The fact that I was limping and had a bandaged forehead and hand could only add to my aura. I wanted something from these people and, if sympathy would help me get it, I was prepared to look like I needed it.

As I opened the door, Hadley Collins got up and walked toward me, taking my hands in hers as she led me into the room and the head of the table. It was a moment to savor. The other members, except for one person, started to applaud. Only Edd Wells remained motionless, suddenly finding a great need to peruse the papers on the table in front of him.

Being a Leo, I, of course, loved the attention. Hadley fussed over me until I was seated, then raised her hands to quiet the others.

"As you can tell by our greeting, Tom, we're glad to have you back with us. Never has anyone in the history of this university done so much to fulfill a committee assignment."

Laughter rippled through the room and various members nodded their heads in agreement.

"We've seen the completed ads and I, for one, think they're great. If they don't bring new students rolling through the gates, I don't know what will."

Again, the others nodded and there was another round of applause.

"I wanted to give you the chance to say something."

She sat down and, for effect, I struggled to my feet, appearing, to all the world, to be on the verge of collapse.

"Thanks so much to all of you for your cards and phone calls. You too, Edd."

Wells' face got red as he continued to look at his folder.

"I'd like to ask that we not forget a wonderful person who so wanted to be part of this ad campaign—Emily Morgan. I think her father is planning to set up a scholarship fund for freshmen in her honor—the very people these ads are trying to attract to the university."

Again, there were murmurs of approval around the table.

"I also wanted to ask for your agreement for Hadley to ask the president to double the advertising budget so these ads can run on television longer and in more cities. Every study of advertising effectiveness I know about has found that repetition—however irritating it is to viewers—re-enforces an ad message best."

I turned to Hadley, who stood up.

"I'm not going to ask for a formal vote here," she said, "but for a consensus. Do you agree to Tom's request?"

One by one, members nodded their heads—Dean Conway, Liz Stein, Carson Bradshaw, Skip Olson, and Margaret Rollins. At first, Edd Wells remained motionless. When all eyes turned on him, however, he finally nodded his assent

"Good. Thank you all very much," Hadley said. "There is only one other order of business."

"This is probably as good a time as any to talk about our next meeting," said Skip Olson. The others reached for their Palm Pilots. "I'm out for two weeks. Going with the president to Hawaii for alumni meetings."

"I'm in California for a fashion retailing seminar," added Edna Blandings Conway.

"Why are we looking at our whatcha macallits? Carson Bradshaw was still lost.

"I'm trying to get a visa to go to the Feminist Socialist Congress in Havana," said Liz Stein. "I'll be gone for a month."

Hadley looked amused and once again raised her hand to quiet the din.

"Just a minute, people," she shouted. "Let me say something. We won't need another meeting in the foreseeable future. Our work is done—at least for now. We won't disband but there is no need for us to get together on a regular basis any more."

The members looked relieved and slightly chagrined at their various outbursts. They immediately turned off their PDAs and stood.

"Before we go, there is one other thing to do . . . Edd."

She motioned toward Wells who very reluctantly got up and pulled a wrapped package from under the table. I could tell he didn't want to do whatever he was about to do but had been forced into the role of gift presenter very much against his will. He walked to the front of the room and handed a box to me, a weak smile on his face. I accepted it and shook his hand, then got to my feet. Hadley started talking.

"We wanted to show you our appreciation for truly exceptional work. We noticed you didn't have one of these, so go ahead and open it."

I smiled gratefully and tore off the paper, revealing a white box. I pulled off the lid.

"Thank you so much. I'll treasure this always."

There in the box was my very own Palm Pilot.

Ron Lovell had a career as a magazine writer in New York, Denver, Houston, and Los Angeles before joining the journalism staff at Oregon State University. The author of thirteen textbooks and hundreds of magazine article writes full-time in Gleneden Beach, Oregon. Sunstone Press published his first two novels in the Thomas Martindale Series in 2002 and 2003.

Printed in the United States
19559LVS00005B/130-183

9 780865 344259